The Great Spaniel Escape

A Story of an English Cocker Spaniel

DOG TALES #4

The Great Spaniel Escape

A STORY OF AN
ENGLISH COCKER SPANIEL

BY COLEEN HUBBARD

Illustrations by Lori Savastano

**AN
APPLE
PAPERBACK**

SCHOLASTIC

New York   Toronto   London   Auckland   Sydney
Mexico City   New Delhi   Hong Kong

For Larry, who had the first idea.

If you purchased this book without a cover, you should be aware that this book is stolen property. It was reported as "unsold and destroyed" to the publisher, and neither the author nor the publisher has received any payment for this "stripped book."

No part of this publication may be reproduced in whole or in part, or stored in a retrieval system, or transmitted in any form or by any means, electronic, mechanical, photocopying, recording, or otherwise, without written permission of the publisher. For information regarding permission, write to Scholastic Inc., Attention: Permissions Department, 555 Broadway, New York, NY 10012.

ISBN 0-590-18978-6

Copyright © 1999 by Coleen Hubbard. Illustrations copyright © 1999 by Scholastic Inc. All rights reserved. Published by Scholastic Inc. SCHOLASTIC and logos are trademarks and/or registered trademarks of Scholastic Inc. APPLE PAPERBACKS and the APPLE PAPERBACKS logo are trademarks and/or registered trademarks of Scholastic Inc.

12 11 10 9 8 7 6 5 4 3 2 1   9/9 0 1 2 3 4/0

Printed in the U.S.A.   40
First Scholastic printing, March 1999

CONTENTS

ONE

L & R Leash Service

Rachel Farley watched as her best friend practically flew out the back door of her house and ran for the shade of the orange tree where Rachel was sitting. Lindy Martinez flopped down beside her, breathing a sigh of relief.

"Are you ready?" Rachel asked. "What took you so long?"

"I had to clean my room," Lindy said with a sigh. "I've been so busy with dogs this week that I could hardly find my bed under all the mess."

Lindy quickly pulled her long black hair into a ponytail and secured it with a green elastic band. "Now we can get going." Her dark eyes shone with excitement as she fastened her sandals and adjusted her sunglasses.

"It's so hot already," said Rachel. "My mom said it's supposed to reach ninety-five degrees again!" Rachel's fair skin itched from the sun-block her mom had insisted she apply before going outside. She wished she had creamy brown skin like Lindy — skin that glowed all summer long without burning or itching or getting covered with freckles.

"Maybe we can go to the beach after we're done with our afternoon shift," Lindy suggested. "Will your mom let you?"

Rachel pushed her red hair behind her ears and considered this. "I hope so. We've hardly been to the beach at all this summer and June's almost over."

"But think how much money we've already earned! L & R Leash Service has brought in sixty dollars this month. If we keep this up, by the end of summer we'll each have almost a *hundred* dollars!"

"And we'll be able to take horseback riding lessons," Rachel added. "Just like we've always dreamed about!"

"And it was all your idea," Lindy said, smiling at her friend. "You were a genius to suggest L & R Leash — the best dog-walking service in Cove Beach."

The initials *L* and *R* stood, of course, for Lindy and Rachel. Rachel had come up with the idea after her mother told her that if she wanted to take riding lessons, she'd have to earn part of the money herself over summer vacation. Rachel had thought and thought about what she could do — she was too young to baby-sit and selling lemonade never earned very much. Then one day when she and Lindy were walking their family pets around the block, a neighbor asked if they'd be interested in walking her dog, too. Since both girls loved dogs, the idea for a dog-walking service seemed like a great fit.

"I didn't know we'd be this busy, though," admitted Rachel. "I thought we'd each walk our own dog, plus maybe two or three others."

"And now we're walking eight dogs total!" Lindy shook her head in wonder at the success of their small business. "Not bad for a couple of ten-year-olds."

Just then, Lindy's little sister twirled her way outside, outfitted in her favorite pink tutu, tights, and ballet slippers. She danced over to the older girls and spun around in circles, finishing in a low, dramatic bow.

Rachel clapped and cheered and reached over to give the five-year-old a hug. "You're such a good dancer, Shelby! When are you going to start your lessons?"

"I don't know," the little girl answered. "I have to ask Mommy."

"Mom said you're not having ballet lessons until you can learn to keep your hair brushed," Lindy teased. "Ballet dancers have to keep their hair pulled back in a bun, not hanging all wild in their face."

Shelby narrowed her dark eyes and put her hands on her hips, staring at her big sister. "Lindy, you're mean! And I hate you! I wish Rachel was my sister because she's nice!"

"She's nice to you because she doesn't have to live with you," Lindy said with a laugh. "She'd get tired of sharing a house with someone who eats, sleeps, and lives in her tutu and is always leaping off the couch."

Shelby immediately burst into tears and ran back to the house, wailing for her mom. Lindy watched her go, rolling her eyes at Rachel. "She cries if you say anything to her. And then she goes and gets Mom, and then Mom gets mad at me."

Sure enough, Lindy's mom came outside, dressed for work in a pale linen dress and summer sandals. She hooked a pair of silver earrings in her ears as she walked over to the girls. "Lindy, were you teasing your sister again?" she asked. "Good morning, Rachel," she added with a smile.

"Good morning," said Rachel. She looked admiringly at Jill Martinez, who appeared so crisp and cool, despite the soaring temperature.

"I just told her that ballet dancers have to keep their hair neat," Lindy said innocently. "She cries if you look at her."

"She's at that sensitive age," Jill replied. "You were the same way."

"She cries less than my little brother," offered Rachel. "You haven't heard crying until you've spent a few minutes at our house." Rachel's brother, Luke, was just three months old.

"How *is* that little sweetie?" Jill asked. "And how's your mom doing?"

"Everyone's fine," Rachel said. "They both sleep a lot. So I'm glad I have dogs to walk or I'd be pretty bored."

"Speaking of dogs," said Lindy, "we should get going." She looked down at the list in her hand. "For our nine o'clock walk we have the Mitchells' dog, the Harrisons' dog, the Alverezes' dog, and my dog. This afternoon we have the Gordons', the Brockbanks', the Paddocks', and *your* dog."

Jill shook her head in wonder. "I don't know how you keep track of all those dogs."

"We haven't lost one yet!" Rachel said.

"Well," said Jill, "I'm proud of you. You've really made a go of this dog-walking business. And now *I* have to get to work. Lindy, Mrs. West is inside with Shelby. Check with her before you leave. And wave to me when you pass by the mayor's office, okay?"

"Okay," Lindy agreed. "It'll be around ten o'clock."

Lindy's mom worked as the press secretary to the mayor of the town of Cove Beach, California. And in a funny twist of fate, Rachel's stepfather, Tom Bates, also worked for the mayor, as her top aide. In fact, the location of the mayor's office, right on Main Street next to Cove Beach Park, was the reason both sets of parents had agreed to let the girls walk dogs in the park. They knew that they'd be able to keep an eye on their daughters, and help out if they were ever needed. At around ten in the morning and two in the afternoon, Lindy's mom and Rachel's stepdad would stop what they were doing and wave from the large front window of Mayor Gretta Mussel's office.

* * *

After the girls had collected the four dogs for their morning shift, they headed for the park in the center of town. It was only three blocks away, but the scorching heat made every block seem like a stretch of the Sahara Desert. And it wasn't only the humans who felt the heat — most of the dogs seemed to lack their usual boundless energy, too.

Lindy walked her family pet, Sam, and a white Poodle named Bubbles. Since Sam was a small, brown mixed-breed dog, he walked well with Bubbles and didn't try to pull too much on the leash. But Rachel struggled with her two charges: a yellow Lab named Mook and a beautiful red Irish Setter named Gloria.

Though Mook and Gloria were about the same size, Mook was much more eager and enthusiastic. He wanted to run and play, while Gloria was happy to walk at an even pace, sniffing the grass as she went along. Mook pulled and tugged at the leash, excited to reach the park where he knew he would get to play chase with a yellow tennis ball.

"This isn't working," said Rachel, coming to a stop on the warm sidewalk. "Sit, Mook. Sit, Gloria."

Both dogs obeyed, plopping down and looking up at Rachel as if to say, *Okay, now what?*

"Do you want to switch dogs?" Lindy asked.

"Mook is pulling my shoulder out of its socket," Rachel explained. "And Gloria likes to poke along and smell every blade of grass."

Lindy reached inside the fanny pack that was hooked around her waist. She brought out four small treats and gave one to each of the dogs. "Have a snack while we figure this out." All four dogs happily munched away, distracted for the moment.

"Everyone thinks we have this really easy job," mused Rachel, "but they don't understand how hard it is to get four dogs and two people to the park and back, in the blazing sun, with all the tourists clogging the streets."

"I know," agreed Lindy. "Doesn't it seem that by the end of June, Cove Beach has about twice as

many people crammed into the same amount of space?"

"That's why my mom hardly ever lets us go near the beach until right around dinner, when all the tourists go back to their cottages and hotels. Then you can at least walk across the sand without tripping over someone."

Lindy reached down to pat Bubbles on her soft white head. "I miss the beach. We practically lived there last summer, remember?"

"I know. It's a good thing we both love dogs."

"True," said Lindy. "You have to admit, we've been lucky with our clients. We haven't had a problem dog or a fussy dog or a mean dog. You're all sweethearts, aren't you?" She leaned down to give the dogs pats on their heads and chests.

"Yes, they are," Rachel agreed. "Look at them — a white dog, a yellow dog, a red dog, and a brown dog. We have the rainbow assortment."

Lindy wiped a thin film of sweat from her forehead and looked at her watch. "We should get going."

"I have an idea," said Rachel. "What if I trade you Gloria for Sam? Because even though Gloria is loads bigger, she walks at about the same pace as Bubbles. And Mook and Sam are both faster."

"It's worth a try." The girls exchanged leashes and straightened out the four dogs. Now they each had a big dog and a small dog.

"That's it! Good girls!" said Lindy. Her dogs paced happily beside her, with no tugging or lagging behind.

But together, Mook and Sam were a whirlwind. They walked so fast that Rachel had to jog a little to keep up. "Meet you at the park!" she called back to Lindy as the dogs pulled her along. "See you at the fountain!"

Cove Beach Park was a beautiful, shaded jewel in the center of town, a perfect escape from the hot, sandy beach and the crowded streets. It had dense, lush flower gardens, tall trees, winding paths, and a huge fountain. The fountain was circled by iron benches where both townspeople and tourists rested, read the paper, or watched the activity in the busy park.

By the time Lindy reached the fountain, Rachel was already there, letting Mook and Sam have a much-needed drink of cool water. No one seemed to mind if dogs used the fountain as their own private source of refreshment — a regular drinking fountain for humans stood just across the way.

"Hey, slowpoke," teased Rachel. "We thought you'd never get here."

"It's true," said Lindy. "Gloria likes to take her time. But here we are." Gloria and Sam helped themselves to a drink from the fountain, while Mook pulled on the leash.

Rachel petted the coarse yellow hair on his ear. "You're ready to play ball, aren't you?" She took a yellow tennis ball out of her pocket and unhooked Mook from his leash. "Will you take Sam while I throw the ball for Mook? Then we'll switch while you play with Sam."

"Sure," said Lindy. "It's a good thing that Bubbles and Gloria aren't into balls. We'd really be in trouble." She put the remaining dogs in a sit position and watched as Rachel tossed the ball to the happy Lab.

A few minutes later, Rachel brought back Mook and the very wet tennis ball. "That's the only part of the job I don't really like — the slobbery ball when Mook's finished."

"That, and being the official pooper-scoopers." Lindy finished cleaning up after Sam and deposited the plastic bag in a nearby trash can.

After Lindy tossed the ball to Sam a dozen times, Rachel asked what time it was.

Lindy glanced at her watch. "Just about time to head back. My mom and your dad will be waiting at the window to wave at us."

Rachel still couldn't get used to hearing the word *dad* when people referred to her stepfather. Her own father had died when she was very small, and it had always been just Rachel and her mom, Gwen. Then, two years ago, Gwen and Tom had married, and now Rachel had a new brother. Her family had grown from two to four! And though

Rachel loved Tom, she always called him Tom. The word *dad* just didn't seem to roll off her tongue. Luckily, Tom and Gwen were easygoing — they said it didn't matter what you called people; only what was in your heart mattered.

"Hey," said Lindy. "Are you daydreaming?"

"I guess I was. Sorry. I think the heat is getting to my brain."

The park was becoming crowded as children and adults and senior citizens looked for a cool place to rest. The girls had to dodge Frisbees and blankets and strollers as they left with the dogs.

"Let's make a promise, Lindy," Rachel said as she tried to navigate Mook and Sam around a group of day campers making kites. "Let's promise not to take on any more canine clients."

"Are you worried that we can't handle any new business? You *are* the official worrywart of L & R Leash, after all."

Rachel laughed, even though it was partly true. She knew she was usually the one concerned about potential problems. Lindy was more carefree, confident that things would work out fine. "I just want some time to enjoy a little bit of summer before we have to go back to school."

"I know what you mean," said Lindy. "I solemnly promise that I will not take on any more dogs to walk." She stopped long enough to raise her left hand and put her right hand across her heart. "Besides, this weekend is the Fourth of July, and I want to go to the barbecue."

"And don't forget the parade."

"Right," said Rachel. "And the fireworks at the beach."

"It's a promise," Lindy repeated. "NO MORE DOGS!"

TWO

Official Business

"There they are," said Lindy, pointing to the window of the mayor's office. "Our bodyguards."

"Just like clockwork," Rachel added, waving to the two figures. "Four minutes after ten o'clock — on the dot. Do you want to stop and say hi?"

"Sure," said Lindy. "Actually, I have to run inside and use the bathroom. Do you think you can handle all four dogs?"

Rachel nudged her friend playfully. "Sure, no problem. Two dogs, four dogs — what's the difference?"

The girls stopped in front of a pale stucco, two-story building. It had been a house at the turn of the century, but now it was the mayor's office. A sign on the door read GRETTA MUSSEL, MAYOR,

COVE BEACH, CALIFORNIA. Jill Martinez and Tom Bates grinned and waved from the first-floor window.

"Sit, Bubbles. Sit, Gloria," said Lindy. She handed the leashes to Rachel and ran lightly up the steps to the front door.

The four panting dogs blew their hot breath on Rachel's bare legs, like portable heaters. She took a deep breath of salt air, wishing desperately that she was at the beach, only blocks away, plunging into the cool waves. She felt sticky and thirsty, and sorry for the dogs with their covering of fur.

"You guys must be so hot!" she said as she attempted to put Mook and Sam in a sit. Sam obeyed, but Mook still wanted to play. "It must be because you're still a puppy," she said to him. "Wait six months and all you'll want to do is sleep all day, like most dogs!"

Just then Tom came whistling out of the office, hands in his pockets and a smile on his freshly shaven face. He had short gray hair and wore a crisp white shirt with an open collar.

"Morning, honey," he said to Rachel. "How's the dog walking going today?"

"Pretty well. But it sure is hot already!"

"I know," Tom agreed. "Luckily, the air-conditioning inside is working — at least for the moment."

Mook instantly began his sniffing routine — starting at Tom's shoes and working up to the cuffs and knees of his pants. The other dogs stayed sitting, not willing to exert any unnecessary energy.

"What are you doing today?" Rachel asked. "Is Mayor Mussel muscling you around?"

"Well, with all the Fourth of July activities going on this weekend, we're pretty busy. Believe it or not, I was checking to see if we'd ordered enough watermelons for the town barbecue. Pretty important stuff, huh? I have to figure out exactly how many melons will provide just the right amount of seeds for the kids to use in the seed-spitting contest!"

"And how many is that?" Rachel wondered.

"Let's see," said Tom. "I estimated that each

melon has around fifteen hundred seeds, give or take a few. So, if you have thirty melons — well, that's a lot of spitting."

Rachel giggled at Tom. She thought he had a good sense of humor. He always made her laugh — and her mom, too. No matter how crazy or busy things were, Tom could find something to laugh about. He could probably even make ordering watermelons a fun way to spend his morning. Rachel knew she was pretty lucky to have him for a — well, dad! Even if she couldn't seem to call him that.

Lindy reappeared carrying two cans of soda. She handed one to Rachel, who took it gladly and pressed the cold can to her forehead. "Thanks! This is exactly what I need!"

"Are you going to drink it? Or just hold it on your face?"

"I don't know," Rachel admitted. "I'm too hot to decide."

"Looks like you'd better get these dogs out of the sun," observed Tom. "The little white one is panting so hard it looks as if her tongue is going to fall out."

"Bubbles," said Lindy. "They'll be glad to get back to their backyards and air-conditioned houses. I know I will."

Just as the girls had straightened out all the leashes and were ready to leave, Jill came running out after them. "Wait!" she called. "Hold on a second!"

"What?" asked Lindy, turning back. "Don't tease Shelby, right?"

"No," said Jill with a laugh. "But that's not a bad idea. Listen, Mayor Mussel wants to talk to both of you."

"She does?" Rachel asked.

"She does?" Tom repeated.

"Yes," Jill said. "But not right now. She's on an important call. Can you girls come back here after you've delivered your dogs? I'll bring in some lunch."

"What's this about, Mom?" Lindy asked.

"Gretta wouldn't say. She was very mysterious," said Jill. "But she said to tell you it's 'official business.' "

"Official business?" Rachel turned to Lindy and stared. What could Mayor Mussel possibly want with the two of them? "Do you know, Tom?"

"Haven't got a clue. Unless she wants another opinion on how many melons we need for the seed-spitting contest."

"Tom, is it okay with you if Rachel comes back here for lunch?" asked Jill.

"I think so," Tom said. Then he turned to Rachel and added, "Unless Mom has any plans for you that I don't know about."

Rachel shook her head. "She said she had to take Luke to the pediatrician. Until she comes home, I'm supposed to stay with Lindy and Mrs. West."

"That's right!" Jill remembered. "So I'll call Mrs. West and let her know that you'll both be having lunch here at the office."

"What are we having?" Lindy asked. "Not yogurt, please!"

"How about if I go across the street and pick up burritos?" Tom suggested. "With extra cheese and hot sauce?"

"Yum!" said Rachel. "And rice, too. And tortilla chips with guacamole!"

"Now you're talking," Lindy agreed. "All my mom ever eats for lunch is yogurt! Yuck!"

"That's because," Jill explained, "I never have time to eat anything else. The mayor keeps me busy from the minute I walk in until the minute I leave."

"True," Tom sighed. "We don't have much time to slack off."

"I can't believe you want to run for mayor when you know how hard it is, Mom!" Lindy said. "You must be crazy."

"That's not for another year and a half," Jill said, "when Gretta retires. I can't even think about that right now."

"You'll be a great mayor, Jill," Tom said. "You

know the job inside out, from working with Gretta all these years."

"And you're a lot nicer," Rachel added.

"Rachel," Tom said, giving her a warning look. "Let's be polite."

"Well, it's true," said Lindy, coming to her friend's defense. "Even if she is my mom, I think she's a hundred times nicer than Mayor Muscle!" Lindy flexed her arm and made a fist.

"I have to defend Gretta," Tom said. "She works hard, and she's tough, but that's why Cove Beach is such a great place to live. And we'd better stop talking about her, since she could join us at any moment."

Rachel smiled up at Tom, who never said a bad word about anyone. He was so kind that Rachel sometimes wondered if there were something wrong with him. Didn't he ever get mad? Was he ever grumpy? Her mom said that some people were just naturally positive and cheerful. But Rachel wasn't sure about that, since she had plenty of tired, crabby, frustrating times herself.

Like right now, standing in the hot sun with four wriggling dogs and the mayor of Cove Beach waiting to talk to her about "official business."

After the dogs had been delivered to their homes, Rachel and Lindy turned right around to retrace their steps to the mayor's office.

"What do you think she wants?" Rachel asked. "Do you think we're in trouble?"

"Why would we be in trouble?"

"I don't know." Rachel shrugged. "Maybe you have to have a permit or something to walk dogs. Or some kind of license to run a business."

Lindy stopped in the middle of the sidewalk and laughed at her friend. "Stop being such a worrywart! You worry too much for a kid!"

"That's what my mom and Tom always say," Rachel admitted. "But I can't help it. I was born this way."

"Maybe you have the worry gene."

"The what?"

"The worry gene," Lindy explained. "My dad

told me about it. He read it in one of the nine hundred magazines he subscribes to."

Lindy's dad, Rob, was a lawyer who worked for himself in a small office attached to the Martinezes' home. Every morning he would get dressed, have his breakfast, and walk ten steps outside his house. Then he would be at work! At least, when he wasn't driving around the countryside to visit the people in very small towns who needed his services.

Rachel thought it was cool that Lindy's dad was a lawyer who helped people. But the thing she liked the most about Rob Martinez was that on the weekends he taught in-line skating classes. He was an incredible blader — fast and skilled. Practically everyone in town had either learned the sport from him, or sent their kids to practice with him. It was a familiar sight to see Rob Martinez whizzing through the streets of Cove Beach wearing his black shorts, pads, and bright purple helmet.

"So, what about the worry gene?" Rachel asked.

"Well, this article said that scientists have located a gene in some people that causes them to worry. Just the way some people have blue eyes and some people have freckles."

"And what are you supposed to do if you have it?" Rachel wondered. "Worry about having it?"

"Nothing. Just be aware of it, so you can realize that sometimes you're worrying out of habit and not because something bad may happen."

"I bet," said Rachel, "that *you* don't have the worry gene."

Lindy laughed and shook her head. "I don't think so. I think I have the *unworry* gene, which is also a problem. Sometimes I don't worry when I *should* worry."

"Like not worrying that we have too many dogs to handle?" Rachel asked lightly.

"Right," said Lindy. "But so far, so good. L & R Leash hasn't made a mistake yet!"

Lindy's enthusiasm and confidence were contagious. It was hard to keep hold of your worry when you were around such sunny people as

Lindy and Tom. But Rachel still couldn't figure out what Mayor Mussel wanted with them. She usually didn't say more than hello to the girls when they stopped by to see their parents.

"Do you think Mayor Mussel is a little scary?" Rachel asked.

"Sort of," said Lindy. "She's very serious, and when she looks at you, her eyes never blink."

"I know. She never smiles. And she wears those suits with the little bow ties."

"But," said Lindy, "my mom says she's actually very nice when you get to know her. And she really cares about our town."

"Tom says the same thing. He says he thinks she might be lonely, because she lives alone and her kids are all grown up."

"Don't forget her dog," said Lindy. "She loves that little black dog like a baby!"

"It's a Cocker Spaniel, isn't it?" Rachel asked.

Lindy nodded. "Named Fannie. Can you believe some of the weird things people name their animals?"

Rachel laughed, remembering her next-door neighbors. "The Hansons have a cat named Missy Poo!"

"Oh, yuck!" cried Lindy. "And get this — my cousin Tim named his dog Red because it has a red coat!"

"No imagination! If it had spots he'd probably name it Spot."

"Or," said Lindy, "if it had a white tip on its tail it would be Tippy!"

Rachel laughed even louder. "Or if it were a big dog he'd call it Big!"

The girls went on joking, not even realizing they were almost back at the mayor's office. But then Rachel spotted Gretta Mussel, standing out on the steps, her arms crossed. She was staring right at them!

Rachel shushed Lindy with a little nudge to the elbow. Then she raised her hand in greeting. "Hello!" she called, trying to keep her voice steady and calm.

"I've been waiting for you," Mayor Mussel responded. "I thought you'd never get here."

"We had to take all of our dogs back," Lindy explained lightly.

"Well, follow me," said the mayor, not even a trace of a smile on her face. "We have important business to discuss and I don't have a minute to waste."

The girls shared a quick glance and then followed the mayor into her chilly, air-conditioned office.

THREE

Fannie Makes Nine

"Please sit down," said Mayor Mussel formally. She indicated two stiff gray chairs arranged in front of her huge wooden desk, which was piled high with files and stacks of paper.

Lindy and Rachel each took a seat, watching as the mayor closed the heavy door to her office. There was a moment of awkward silence as they waited for her to explain her "official business."

Mayor Mussel folded her hands on top of the desk and stared at the girls through the glasses perched at the end of her nose. Her gray hair was pulled back into a tight bun, and she wore tiny pearl earrings. As usual, she was dressed in a navy suit with a floppy red silk bow tie. She looked so businesslike and *hot*. Especially when compared with all the people walking past the window dressed in shorts and sandals and wide-brimmed summer hats.

Finally she cleared her throat and began. "I understand you two young ladies have formed a small business this summer."

Oh, no! thought Rachel. *We were supposed to get a license!*

"That's right," Lindy answered with confidence. "L & R Leash."

"Which stands for what?" Mayor Mussel asked, not taking her eyes off of Lindy.

"The initials stand for Lindy and Rachel, and the leash part is because we walk dogs." Lindy turned to smile at Rachel, as if to say, *See, everything is fine!*

"And your business is successful, I gather," said the mayor, "judging from the large gaggle of dogs I see outside my window each day." The corners of her mouth turned down to form a slight frown.

"I'm sorry if the dogs bother you," Rachel said.

"We just stop to wave to Lindy's mom and my — Tom."

"I'm never bothered by dogs," said the mayor. "Dogs are one of the passions of my life. Especially Fannie."

"She's cute," said Lindy with a smile. "I saw her once when you came by our house. She was sleeping in your car."

"Yes, well — " Mayor Mussel stammered. "I usually bring her inside with me, but she's a little afraid of — small children."

"Afraid of children?" Rachel couldn't believe her ears. Most dogs absolutely loved children. At least all the dogs she'd known.

"Well, you see," Mayor Mussel explained, "she hasn't been around them much. My own children are grown and I live alone, as you know. Fannie and I have our own routine — our walks, our drives in the car, our relaxing time at home."

Rachel noticed how the mayor's voice and features softened as she thought about her dog. "But why is Fannie *afraid* of children? Did something happen to her?"

"Actually," sighed Mayor Mussel, "it did. She's only two years old, and last Halloween she ran out the door when I opened it for some trick-or-treaters. Several boys dressed as pirates chased her around and poked at her with their swords. She was terrified!"

"That's awful!" said Rachel. And she meant it. It made her furious to think that people teased and mistreated animals — even if they claimed it was all in fun. Dogs deserved kindness and respect. Whenever Rachel saw someone teasing an animal, she always asked them to stop.

"I hate it when people do that," Lindy agreed. "Even my little sister, who's only five, knows how to treat dogs and cats."

The mayor took a deep breath and nodded at the girls. "I've been watching you for the past week or so. I'm very impressed with how you care for the dogs you walk."

Rachel smiled with relief and Lindy nudged her as if to say, *Told you so!*

"And," continued Mayor Mussel, "I called you here today to offer you a job with my own sweet Fannie. The dearest dog in the state of California!"

"You did?" Lindy's voice sounded surprised, as if the mayor had asked her to stand on her head and recite the alphabet backward.

Mayor Mussel stood up. She held a pad of paper and a pen in her hand. "I'm going to be so busy from now until the Fourth of July weekend is over. All the picnics and parades and official duties! And my housekeeper is leaving on vacation. I need someone to walk Fannie until my housekeeper returns on July third."

"We can do it!" Lindy said. "No problem!"

Rachel gave Lindy a swift kick in the foot, trying to stop her from talking. They'd agreed not to take on any more animals. L & R Leash was at full capacity! To walk even one more dog would be foolish.

"Wait," said Mayor Mussel, holding up her hand. "It's not just walking. You see, Fannie is used to a very specific routine. And when her routine is altered at all, poor thing, she gets a very upset stomach. And when that happens — well, it's not pretty."

"Mayor Mussel," began Rachel, "we really appreciate your asking us, and maybe if we didn't already — "

But just then Jill knocked softly at the door and poked her head inside. "Sorry to interrupt."

"Hi, Mom!" said Lindy.

"Hello, honey. Gretta, the superintendent of schools is on line one. He says it's very important."

"I should take that," said the mayor. "If you girls will excuse me for just a moment, we can continue our discussion when I'm finished with this call."

"Tom has your lunch in the conference room," Jill told the girls. "Why don't we go eat and leave Gretta to her call."

The girls followed Jill to the empty conference room, where Tom had arranged a wonderful feast. Spread out on the long table were foil containers of burritos, rice, beans, guacamole, and salsa.

"I'll go get Tom," said Jill. "Dig in."

But Rachel wasn't going to touch a bite until she and Lindy had agreed about Fannie. "We can't take on any more dogs! You promised just an hour ago!"

"I know," said Lindy. "But this is Mayor Mussel we're talking about. Our parents' boss. We can't say no to her!"

"Why not? We'll just tell her we have too many dogs already, but maybe next year."

"Don't you see?" said Lindy. "It's not that simple. First of all, our parents *work* for the mayor."

"So?"

"So," said Lindy, as if she were talking to her little sister, "if we keep the mayor happy, then she'll be nice to my mom and your dad, and *they'll* be happy."

Rachel was silent. What Lindy said had some

truth to it. Rachel had often heard Tom say, "When Gretta's happy, everyone's happy."

"Do you see what I mean?"

"Yes," Rachel admitted slowly.

"And don't forget — my mom wants to be the next mayor, and she keeps saying she needs Mayor Mussel to endorse her campaign."

"What does that mean, exactly?" Rachel asked.

"It means she needs Mayor Mussel to say, in the newspaper, that my mom would be the best candidate to become the next mayor of Cove Beach."

"Well, she would be. That's the truth."

"I know. And you know. But the rest of Cove Beach needs to hear it from Mayor Mussel next year."

"I'm starting to see your point," said Rachel. "It would be kind of — awkward to say no."

"Right! And here's the good part," said Lindy. "Think about how rich Mayor Mussel must be. She lives in that big glass house up above the beach. And she has a housekeeper — "

"And that fancy car!" finished Rachel.

"So," said Lindy with her mischievous smile, "think about the big tip she might give us. And then think about signing up for riding lessons this fall. Think about riding that chestnut horse you're always dreaming about, down at the stables — "

"Okay! Okay!" Rachel said with a laugh. "You win! You've convinced me. But how are we going to manage nine dogs?"

Lindy blew a stream of air up toward her bangs and tapped her fingers on the table. "I don't know yet. But we'll manage."

"We can't take more than two dogs each at a time. We don't have enough arms. We weren't octopuses the last time I checked."

"We'll just have to do more shifts."

"But we already have a morning and an afternoon shift. And we haven't been to the beach all week." Rachel thought fleetingly of the feel of soft white sand on her bare toes and the salty taste of the sea. . . .

"Aren't you girls eating?" Tom asked as he entered the conference room. "I thought you were starving."

"We are." Rachel smiled up at Tom. "We were just about to start." She picked up a paper plate and began loading it with the spicy food.

"So, I'm dying to know, girls — what did the mayor want with the two of you?"

Lindy picked up a plate and went for the guacamole. "She wants us to walk Fannie until the third of July."

"She's hiring you?" Tom let out a low whistle of admiration. "You should be flattered. She's very picky about her dog."

"I could sort of tell," Rachel admitted. "She didn't really finish explaining all the stuff we have to do."

"Oh, she will. She'll write it all down on a list."

Sure enough, when Mayor Mussel bustled into the conference room a few minutes later, she was holding a pad of paper. "Can we make this a working lunch? I have a list."

"What?" said Lindy, looking confused.

Tom chuckled and explained. "She means, can you eat and finish your meeting at the same time?"

"Sure," Rachel said. But she could feel herself losing interest in the piles of food.

The mayor sat down and adjusted her glasses. "Now, is either of you familiar with the English Cocker Spaniel?"

Lindy thought for a moment and shrugged. "Not exactly."

"Well, they are wonderful dogs. They came from Spain originally, which is where the name *spaniel* is derived from."

"No kidding?" Tom asked with great sincerity.

"They were originally bred to hunt woodcock," Mayor Mussel continued. "Which explains where the second part of the name comes from — *cocker.*"

"Interesting," Rachel murmured, trying to be polite.

"Yes, and because they are hunting dogs, they need brisk exercise every day. Brisk!"

Rachel gulped at the word *brisk*. She thought

about Mook and Sam pulling her down the street, and Gloria poking along, sniffing every blade of grass. Not to mention her own dog, Coach, an ancient Collie — twelve years old! — with a bad back leg. He had a hard time walking with another dog at his side.

"No problem," put in Lindy. "We take all our dogs for two walks each day."

"But in addition to the walks," said the mayor, "she needs to be combed thoroughly each day. A spaniel's coat needs special care. And though Fannie is very devoted and friendly, she requires a certain amount of firmness to offset her independent streak."

"Sure thing," said Lindy. She shot Rachel a quick glance that seemed to say, *How long is this list of dog duties going to be?!*

"Now, Fannie loves to play, and because of her retrieving ability, she likes a good game of catch each day. She can find her ball no matter where it ends up — the bushes, under the fence — "

Before she could finish, Jill walked in carrying

a special delivery envelope. "These contracts from the caterer for the Fourth of July picnic just arrived. They need your signature right away."

The mayor snapped to attention. "I've been waiting for those."

"How's lunch, girls?" Jill asked, completely unaware of what was going on.

"Fine," they answered at the same time, avoiding any further comments.

Mayor Mussel stood up and checked her watch. "I'm afraid I'll have to cut our meeting short. And I have so much more to tell you. Let's see . . ."

Rachel tried to catch Lindy's eye, but Lindy was busy finishing her burrito.

"I know!" said the mayor. "How about if I bring Fannie over to meet you girls this evening, after I'm finished with work? That way, you can get to know each other and I can finish going over my list."

"What's this about?" asked Jill, looking from Tom to Lindy to Rachel.

"I've asked the girls to take care of Fannie for a

few days, while I deal with the Fourth of July holiday," Mayor Mussel answered.

Jill beamed, looking proud. "Well, isn't that great? More work for L & R Leash."

"We're the best!" Lindy agreed triumphantly.

"True!" said Rachel, trying to put the right note of enthusiasm into her voice.

"Terrific!" said Tom. "I'm sure Fannie will be a wonderful new addition to the current pack."

Tom and Jill looked so pleased that Rachel began to wonder if maybe things would turn out just fine. *I'm too much of a worrywart,* she thought.

"So," concluded Mayor Mussel. "Should Fannie and I come to your house, Rachel? Or to Lindy's?"

"Come over to our house," Tom offered. "I'm sure Gwen would be happy to see you."

"Seven o'clock?" suggested the mayor.

"That'll be just fine," said Tom.

Mayor Mussel left the room, followed by Tom and Jill.

Lindy looked at Rachel. Then, pretending to

adjust some imaginary glasses, she imitated the mayor's low voice. "Fannie is the best dog in the entire world, if not the universe. She was bred to hunt woodcock in Spain!"

Rachel burst into giggles and had to cover her mouth. But at the same time, she had a sudden realization that sent a shiver down her neck.

Fannie is Mayor Mussel's baby. Just like Luke is my mom's baby. And moms are pretty particular about the care of their babies.

We'd better do an extra good job with this dog!

FOUR

The Fannie Fiasco

"A breeze!" cried Rachel. "I think I feel a breeze off the ocean!"

"Thank goodness!" said Lindy. "Don't move or it might go away."

The two girls lounged in the evening heat on Rachel's front porch, eating ice-cream sandwiches and waiting for Mayor Mussel to arrive. Next to them, in the porch rocker, sat Rachel's mom, Gwen. In her arms, she held baby Luke, who was sweaty and wriggly and fussy.

"Hush," whispered Gwen, rocking back and forth. "It's starting to cool off now. Soon you will sleep."

"You sound as if you're trying to put a spell on him, Mom."

"If only that would work!" Gwen said with a laugh. "Hocus-pocus, sleep till dawn and cry no more!" She waved an imaginary wand in front of the baby's chubby red face. Luke answered with a high-pitched squeal that threatened to turn into a complete breakdown.

Rachel licked the last bite of ice cream off the paper wrapper and stood up. "Hey, Lukey," she cooed, "don't start crying now. Give Mom a break."

"Does he cry all day?" Lindy asked, standing up to join Rachel.

"Sometimes," Gwen admitted. "But mostly it's the evenings that are rough. Good thing he's so cute and we love him so much!"

"Was I like that?" Rachel asked her mom.

Gwen reached a hand up and touched her daughter's cheek. "You were an unbelievably easy baby, Rachel. You rarely cried and you slept through the night when you were six weeks old. You spoiled me — I thought all babies were like that."

"You hear that?" Rachel said to Luke, tickling him under the chin. "You need to follow my example. Sleep is good!"

"I don't know about that," said Lindy. "I *hate* going to sleep. My mom says it's because I'm afraid I might miss out on some fun. Maybe Luke is the same way."

"Maybe so," Gwen said, rocking faster to see if that would help. But Luke only cried harder.

Then Tom came outside to see what he could do. "Maybe I should take him for a drive in the car. Sometimes that puts him right to sleep."

Gwen stood up and handed the baby to Tom. "Be my guest. Take a really LONG drive, and I'll take a really LONG bath." She smoothed her white T-shirt, which was stained with baby drool. "Oh, and maybe I'll change my shirt while I'm at it!"

"Good idea, Mom." Rachel felt sorry for her mom, who didn't get much of a break these days. Taking care of a newborn was a lot of work! Even more work than taking care of dogs.

"Okay, buddy, into your infant seat," Tom said. "You girls waiting for the mayor?"

"Yep," sighed Rachel. "Mayor Mussel is bringing Fannie over to see if she approves of us."

"You don't have to agree to this, you know," Tom told the girls. "Just because she's the mayor doesn't mean you have to say yes to her."

This made Gwen laugh. "Gretta's hard to say no to, from what you've told me over the years!"

"True," Tom admitted, winking at Gwen. "True enough. But the girls don't have to walk Fannie unless they want the business."

And a BIG tip, thought Rachel. *And to make things easier for Lindy's mom and my — Tom. And so Lindy's mom can be elected the next mayor!*

"Well, I'll be inside if you need me," Gwen said to the girls. "I made some lemonade, if you'd like to offer a glass to Gretta when she gets here."

"I'll be back soon," said Tom. "Say good-bye, Luke." He picked up Luke's tiny wrist and moved it back and forth. Then in a high, tiny voice he said, "Bye-bye, Lindy. Bye-bye, big sister."

"Ohhh, Tom!" Rachel drawled, rolling her eyes at Lindy. "What is it about babies that makes grown-ups act so weird and start talking in baby voices?"

"I don't know," Lindy said, "but my parents did it with Shelby all the time."

As Tom pulled his car out of the driveway, Rachel's dog, Coach, wandered around from the backyard. It took great effort for him to climb the three steps to the porch.

"Hey, Coach," Rachel said, petting the collie's soft fur. "How are you, boy? Come over here and sit down. Here you go. That's my sweet doggie!"

Lindy cracked up. "You're doing it, too! You're talking in a baby voice to Coach, just the way our parents talk to babies!"

"I was?" Rachel asked. "I didn't even know."

"It must be some automatic thing. I bet Mayor Mussel does it with Fannie. Wait and see."

Just then the mayor's car pulled into Rachel's driveway. Mayor Mussel emerged from her long, shiny car, still dressed in her suit.

"Hello," she called. "Just give me a minute." She opened the back door of her car and reached inside. "Come here, darling. Come here, my adorable little Fannie-wannie. Come out and meet some new friends. They can't wait to meet the best little spaniel in the whole wide world. Yes, that's right!"

Rachel couldn't believe her ears! Lindy elbowed her, trying not to laugh. Neither girl had ever heard Mayor Mussel use anything but her serious, get-down-to-business voice, and here she was baby-talking a blue streak to her dog!

"Told you," Lindy whispered, trying to compose her face.

Rachel stood up and tried to act mature. "Hello, Mayor Mussel. Hello, Fannie."

Coach barely stirred, too tired from making his way up the porch steps. He looked up with curiosity when the mayor approached with Fannie, but quickly put his head back down on his paws and sighed heavily.

Mayor Mussel carried her black Cocker Spaniel up the steps and sat down in the rocker, cradling the dog. "Shall we have our meeting here, where there's a little breeze?"

"Sure," said Lindy. "Go right ahead."

"Will your dog be bothered by Fannie?"

"Coach?" Rachel laughed. "No. He'll just stay right here and sleep."

"Is he old?"

"Very," said Rachel. "My mom had him as a puppy — before I was born."

Mayor Mussel sighed and held Fannie closer. "I don't even want to think about Fannie growing old. She's my little baby, aren't you, Fannie-wannie?"

Fannie was panting a bit from the heat, but both girls could see that she was a beautiful little dog. Though small and compact, she seemed to have a big personality. Her dark eyes looked very thoughtful.

"I love her coat," Rachel said, petting the thick, silky hair on Fannie's ears.

"I like the way it looks all wavy on her ears and chest," noted Lindy.

"Yes, and that brings up a good point. Spaniels are prone to ear infections. You will need to check her auditory canals each day to be sure they're clean."

"Auditory canals?" Lindy repeated skeptically. "Do you mean ears?"

"Of course I mean ears. Now, I want to talk to you about her feeding schedule."

Rachel began to feel a little nervous. For Coach, she just filled up the dog bowl with kibble and sometimes a little grated cheese. When it was empty the next day, she filled it up again. And she knew Lindy pretty much did the same thing with her dog, Sam. What did the mayor mean by "feeding schedule"?

Mayor Mussel went on to explain how, after Fannie's afternoon walk, she wanted the girls to give the dog a little peeled fruit — because of "certain dietary deficiencies." Lindy and Rachel nodded and smiled and tried to look interested in the long list of instructions involving vitamin supplements, mineral absorption, and fiber content.

"And if you happen to be eating popcorn," the mayor concluded, "you can give her a few nibbles. Popcorn is Fannie's very favorite food. I think she'd do just about anything for popcorn! But not too much — just a handful at most!"

Rachel had a sudden and very comic image of the mayor of Cove Beach sitting in front of her television, watching a movie and eating popcorn with her Cocker Spaniel. She was dying to share it with Lindy, but it would have to wait until later.

I thought we were just walking Fannie, Rachel mused. *What is all this about feeding and popcorn and cleaning out her ears? I think we'd better charge double!*

Suddenly Fannie sat up straight in Mayor Mussel's lap. She tensed her body and cocked her head to follow a sound that wasn't yet apparent to the humans around her.

"She hears something. She has excellent hearing!" said the mayor.

"All dogs have good hearing," Rachel observed politely. "Even old Coach."

As if to prove her point, Coach raised his head slightly and cocked it toward the street.

"It's my sister," Lindy said, peering down the sidewalk. She could see Shelby, three doors down, running toward Rachel's house. And, of course, she was dressed in her pink tights and tutu.

"Shall we continue?" said Mayor Mussel. "I've brought some papers for you to sign."

"Papers?" repeated Lindy.

"What kind of papers?" asked Rachel.

"A contract, of course." Mayor Mussel looked from one girl to the other, as if she were stating the most obvious fact in the world.

"Why would we sign a contract?" Lindy asked.

"Because that's how business is conducted. I'm hiring you to provide certain services, for which I'm paying you a certain amount of money. It's all right here — you can read it over and then we'll all be in agreement. We'll know what to expect of each other. A contract protects both parties."

"We haven't signed a contract with any of the other people we work for," Lindy said. "It's just sort of a — what do you call it? Verbal agreement!"

"But verbal agreements aren't official and — " began Mayor Mussel. But she was interrupted by Shelby, who was calling for her sister.

"Lin-dy!" she hollered. "Oh, Lin-dy!" She ran up to the porch, out of breath. "Mom wants to know when you're coming home."

The minute Fannie saw Shelby in her dancer's costume, she bolted off the mayor's lap and ran toward the car. She sat by the car door, wagging her tail as if to say, *Let me in. Let me away from that strange creature!*

The mayor shot out of the rocker, running down the steps toward her dog. "Fannie, stay! Fannie, I'm coming. Mommy's coming. Everything's all right!"

"Is she the dog's mommy?" Shelby asked with five-year-old innocence.

"Sort of," Lindy answered.

"I'm going to go ask Mommy if she can have a doggie for me. I want a new doggie." Shelby spun down the steps, twirling all over the front yard.

Fannie barked and wagged her tail faster.

Delighted, Shelby danced toward the dog. "Hi, puppy!" she called out. "What's your name?"

"It's Fannie — " Rachel began.

"Keep away!" Mayor Mussel warned in alarm.

"Why?" asked Shelby, freezing in confusion by the car.

Lindy ran over and tried to pick up her little sister. But Shelby was too heavy for her and the two girls toppled over. Rachel couldn't help but giggle, and soon all three girls were howling with laughter. This made Fannie bark even more, which made Shelby shriek with renewed excitement.

Mayor Mussel picked up Fannie and quickly deposited her in the backseat of the car. She slammed the door and leaned against it, looking distraught. "I think we should go. Fannie is very upset."

"I'm sure she's fine," Rachel said soothingly.

"I told you she's not used to children — especially those in costume."

"This isn't a costume," Shelby protested, clutching a handful of pink netting. "I'm a ballet dancer!"

"Maybe," said Lindy helpfully, "Fannie just needs to be around children more, and then she wouldn't be afraid. We could help with that."

"Perhaps," the mayor said, trying to breathe evenly. "But I'm not sure that this arrangement is going to work. You can see how flustered Fannie is." She pushed some stray hairs off her face and took a deep breath.

Maybe it's just the mayor who's flustered, Rachel thought. "Do you want some lemonade?" she asked aloud. If they all sat back down on the porch and had a cool drink, maybe they could work things out.

"No, thank you," Mayor Mussel answered flatly. "I think I should get Fannie home and calm her down."

"She's okay," said Shelby, who had tiptoed over to the car window. "Look, she's putting her paw on the window. She wants to shake my hand!"

Mayor Mussel whipped her head around to check on her dog. "I think you should back away quietly," she whispered to Shelby. "It's nothing personal, but your costume — your *outfit* — has scared her."

"No it didn't," Shelby said. Tears were forming in her big eyes. "I'm not scary! Am I, Lindy?"

"No," said Lindy, coming to give her sister a hug. "You're just fine."

Then Rachel spotted Tom's car turning the corner. She breathed a sigh of relief, knowing he would figure out how to handle the mayor.

Holding his sleeping son, Tom hurried over to say hello. As if he could tell right away that things weren't going well, he gave Mayor Mussel a big smile. "Hello, Gretta. Nice evening, isn't it?"

But Luke chose just that moment to wake up and erupt into a new and even louder burst of crying. He wrinkled up his eyes and howled, tensing every muscle in his tiny body. Fannie, now scratching at the car window, barked along with Luke.

"I'm sorry, but I have to go now," Mayor Mussel said curtly.

"But what about Fannie?" Lindy asked. "Don't you want us to start tomorrow?"

"I think," said the mayor, "that I'd better sleep on this. I'll have my assistant get back to you sometime tomorrow."

It wasn't until she was backing her car out of the driveway that Tom began to laugh.

"What's so funny?" asked Rachel. She didn't think anything was too humorous at the moment.

"She said she'd have her *assistant* get back to you!"

"So?" said Lindy. She, too, was feeling a bit defeated.

"Don't you think that's funny?" Tom asked. "*I* am her assistant!"

Then Rachel and Lindy laughed, too, despite the realization that they'd just, more than likely, been fired by the mayor of Cove Beach!

The Contract

For a while the next day, Lindy and Rachel completely forgot about the fiasco with Mayor Mussel. They pushed aside any thoughts of dogs at all. They were too busy playing in the surf at Cove Beach.

"Here comes a big wave!" shouted Rachel.

Lindy turned around and looked over her shoulder. A huge dark green swell of water pounded toward them. The girls squealed with delight as the wave tossed them gently toward the shore. They floated happily, feeling the late afternoon sun on their faces.

"I'm in heaven," Lindy sighed as she bobbed in the water.

"Me too," agreed Rachel. "It's been too long since we went to the beach."

"At least most people are leaving now, so it's not crowded."

Rachel looked toward shore, where only a few groups of sunbathers remained, spread out on towels and blankets. She spotted her mom lying on a yellow towel, Luke asleep beside her in his umbrella-covered stroller. Rachel was grateful that her mom had agreed to bring them down to the beach. And glad that Gwen was getting at least a few minutes of rest while Luke napped.

"This is the best time to come to the beach," Lindy announced. "I wouldn't set foot here at noon."

"Well, you couldn't, even if you wanted to. At noon we're getting ready for our afternoon dog-walking shift, remember?"

"How could I forget! Hey, Rach?"

"Hmm?" Rachel murmured, floating on her back.

"Do you think Mayor Mussel is still mad at us?"

Rachel sat forward, treading water. "I don't know. But it wasn't exactly our fault."

"You know that and I know that. Even your dad knows that. But obviously Mayor Mussel doesn't know that," said Lindy.

"Maybe it's all for the best, Lindy. I mean, the money would have been nice, but Fannie is an awfully skittish dog."

"True. But isn't she cute?"

"Totally cute," Rachel agreed. "I wonder if . . ."

"What?"

"I just wonder," continued Rachel, "if maybe Mayor Mussel makes Fannie nervous because she's so nervous around her."

"What do you mean?" Lindy ducked her head under the water and pushed back her long dark hair.

"Well, my mom always says that babies and children can pick up on the moods of their parents. Like, if my mom is tense and upset, Luke gets upset, too. And when my mom is really calm, he calms down, too."

"So you think because the mayor is so protective and worried about Fannie, Fannie thinks there's something to be worried about?"

"Exactly," said Rachel. "I mean, anyone who saw your little sister in a pink tutu would know that she was harmless. But the mayor got all excited and then Fannie got excited."

Lindy thought about this, bicycling her feet in the water. "You have a point. When my parents are worried about something, I can usually tell. Then I get worried trying to figure out what they're worried about!"

"I thought you *never* worried, Lindy Martinez!"

Lindy laughed, trying not to gulp any salt water. "Okay, okay. You got me. I worry, on the average, about six times a year — maybe less in leap years."

This made Rachel laugh. "So, I guess that means Mayor Mussel worries about Fannie a hundred times a day."

"Uh-oh!" said Lindy. "Here comes another whopper."

The girls rode the next wave almost all the way back to shore. They crawled out of the sea, laughing and shaking water from their faces and hair. They ran over to Rachel's mom, grabbing dry towels.

Gwen sat up and yawned, looking at her watch. "Having fun?"

Both girls nodded, catching their breath. "It feels so good to be in the water," said Lindy.

"Do you want to go in?" Rachel asked her mom. "We can watch Luke for a few minutes."

Gwen looked over at the sleeping baby, protected from the sun. "That would be great. Come and get me if he starts crying. I'll just be a minute. Rachel — put more sunblock on your face and shoulders."

Rachel and Lindy spread out their towels and watched Gwen run down to the water. "Stay asleep, Luke!" said Rachel, looking over at her brother. "Give Mom a little time in the water."

"Do you think babies or dogs are harder to take care of?" asked Lindy.

"Babies! Unless the dog is a dog like Fannie," offered Rachel. "Even Luke would be easier to take care of than Fannie."

"You know," Lindy mused, "I wish we could do something to help Fannie. She's such a nice dog. I wish we could get her used to other dogs and to children. She'd have so much fun."

"I know," agreed Rachel. "But we lost our chance."

Lindy looked behind her at the row of food vendors near the parking lot. She was suddenly hungry. "Do you want an ice cream? Or some popcorn? That popcorn guy has awesome caramel corn."

"I would love a snow cone. Let's wait for my mom to come back, though. I can't leave Luke."

"Right!" said Lindy, smacking her forehead. "He's being so quiet, I almost forgot he was here."

Rachel listened to the sound of the waves and the seagulls circling overhead. The tips of the waves sparkled white in the low angle of the sun. She could see her mom in her black tank suit, swimming toward shore. Luke continued to sleep — amazing! — and even Lindy stretched out and closed her eyes. Rachel felt relaxed and peaceful and let her mind drift off to thoughts of horses and stables and learning, finally, to ride!

But suddenly Luke stirred and began his high-pitched whine. Rachel snapped to attention and Lindy reluctantly sat up.

"Shh," said Rachel, reaching over to rock the stroller gently. "Don't cry, Lukey, don't cry."

"Here comes your mom," said Lindy, pointing in front of her.

But Rachel was staring off to her left, over the top of Luke's stroller. "Oh, no. I don't believe it!"

"What?"

"Look who's coming!"

Lindy followed Rachel's gaze. "Mayor Mussel?"

"Who else would dress in a business suit to come to the beach?"

The mayor approached the girls, holding a briefcase in one hand and Fannie in the other. She waddled in the sand, trying to keep her balance in high-heeled shoes.

"She looks like a penguin!" whispered Lindy.

"Shhh," Rachel warned. "She'll hear us."

Luke's whine had turned into a full-fledged wail by the time Gwen returned. She scooped him up and held him next to her.

"Mom, you'll get him all wet!"

"I know," said Gwen, "but he's probably sopping wet, anyway. And I don't want him to really start howling."

"Especially with Princess Fannie approaching!" said Lindy.

"Who?" asked Gwen, rocking Luke in her arms.

"The mayor's dog, Fannie. And the mayor," Rachel explained.

"Uh-oh," said Gwen. "Maybe I should take Luke and feed him in the car. I'll meet you girls there. And will you bring the stroller and towels, Rach?"

"Sure," said Rachel, wishing her mom would stay. She was just the tiniest bit afraid of Mayor Mussel. Especially after what had happened the night before.

Hurrying toward the parking lot with the shrieking Luke, Gwen waved at the mayor. The girls stood up as Mayor Mussel came to a stop by Luke's vacated stroller.

"Hello, girls," said the mayor.

"Hi." Rachel smiled.

"Hey, Fannie!" added Lindy. She reached a hand out to pet Fannie, and Fannie responded with a quick, happy lick on Lindy's wrist.

"I'm sorry to bother you while you're off duty. But Tom told me I might find you here."

Rachel nodded and smiled, looking at Lindy for encouragement. But Lindy kept her attention focused on the adorable spaniel who squirmed against the mayor's stiff suit.

"After serious consideration, I've decided to go ahead and hire you to care for Fannie. I know you'll do a good job. I have the contract in my briefcase."

Lindy looked surprised. "What made you change your mind?"

The mayor hugged Fannie tighter. "I know you

didn't mean to startle Fannie last night. And sometimes, well — I'm overprotective. But I can't help it. If anything ever happened to my darling Fannie, I just don't think I could go on!"

"Oh," soothed Rachel, "don't worry. Everyone feels that way about their dog. Right, Lindy?"

"Right! Besides my family and Rachel, I love my dog, Sam, more than anything."

"I knew you'd understand," sniffed the mayor. "I know you love dogs and that you'll do a good job with Fannie. You'll just have to promise to keep her away from children."

"But that's impossible!" said Rachel. "This town is full of children. Especially in the summer. And both Lindy and I have siblings. And — "

"And we'll do our best," Lindy interrupted.

"Well, that's nice to hear, isn't it, Fannie?" Mayor Mussel gave Fannie several smacking kisses on her head, which made Fannie's tail wag happily.

"We need to get back to my mom," Rachel reminded Lindy.

"I'm almost finished," said the mayor. "I'm prepared to offer you twenty-five dollars a day to take care of Fannie. Will that be sufficient?"

Rachel and Lindy were stunned into silence. Twenty-five dollars! That was *ten times* the daily rate they charged their other customers.

"Twenty-five dollars?" Rachel squeaked.

"We'll take it!" said Lindy quickly. "I mean, we'll be happy to take Fannie!"

"Good. Then it's all settled. You'll start tomorrow. Now all we need to do is sign the contract." The mayor handed Fannie to Rachel while she opened her briefcase on the sand. She rustled through some papers until she found what she was looking for.

"Excuse me, Mayor," said Lindy. "But I'm still not sure about the contract. You see, my dad is a lawyer — "

"Then he'll appreciate my drawing up a contract to protect all of us. By all means, have him take a look at it. And call me if he has any ques-

tions. Oh, and I'm prepared to write you a check today."

Rachel held Fannie against her chest, noticing how shiny the dog's coat was. Fannie nestled against her, giving her ear a lick. *She's so sweet!* thought Rachel. *I think we could be really good for her. And twenty-five dollars! I can't believe it!*

Lindy looked at Rachel and shrugged, as if to say: *What harm could it do to sign her silly contract, if it makes her feel better?*

The mayor held out two copies of the contract to Lindy, along with an expensive-looking pen. "It's all spelled out. The money, the dates and times, and the specific duties."

Lindy began to read the contract out loud, pronouncing the strange-sounding legal words just as she'd heard her dad do a hundred times — *hence, thus, hereafter, in perpetuity*. But after a paragraph, she stopped and looked at Rachel with wide eyes, trying to signal that none of it was making sense.

"My mom is probably ready to go," said

Rachel, pointing her thumb toward the parking lot. The words didn't make sense to her, either.

"Okay," said Lindy, looking up. "Let's just sign this." She had a nagging doubt, but she pushed it aside and carefully wrote her name in cursive on the very last page of both copies of the three-page document. Then she handed the pen to Rachel.

"Here," said Rachel. "Take Fannie while I sign."

"Gladly," Lindy said, grinning as she pulled Fannie into her arms. "We're going to be good friends, aren't we, Fannie?"

I hope so, thought Rachel. *I'm trying not to be a worrywart, but what if . . . No, never mind. Everything will be fine. We'll make loads of money, and the mayor will be happy, which means that Jill and Tom will be happy, and maybe we can even help Fannie relax a little. Everything will be fine.*

Rachel signed her name under Lindy's and handed the contract back to the mayor.

"Don't we keep a copy?" Lindy asked the mayor in her best lawyer-like voice.

"Of course," said Mayor Mussel, handing a document to Lindy. "Keep it in a safe place."

Everything will be fine! thought Rachel as they headed for the car, waving good-bye to the adorable Fannie.

Getting to Know Fannie

The very next day, Lindy and Rachel added a third and fourth dog-walking shift — just to accommodate Fannie. The little black spaniel was the only one of nine dogs to have her own private walks in Cove Beach Park.

"So, let me get this straight," said Rachel, who was holding Fannie's pink leash, on which the dog's named was spelled out in gold letters. "At ten we walk our four morning dogs. At noon we walk Fannie and then bring her back to my house because the backyard is fenced and Coach won't bother her. Then we have lunch, walk our afternoon dogs, come back for Fannie and take her for her second walk!"

"You got it," said Lindy. "And don't forget

about playing catch with Fannie, brushing her, and checking her *auditory canals*!"

"Oh, right. We wouldn't want Fannie getting any ear infections."

"This is going to be a long few days!" said Lindy. "When are we going to find time for any fun?"

"Good question," said Rachel.

"But we're going to make a lot of money! And at five P.M. each day we turn Fannie back over to the mayor." Lindy reached down to pet Fannie's soft head. "It won't be so bad."

The girls decided to stop by the drinking fountain in the center of the park and fill up the collapsible water bowl that the mayor had insisted they bring along. "I don't want Fannie drinking out of that statue fountain," she had told the girls. "You have no idea what kinds of bacteria may be growing in there!"

Lindy sat down on a bench with Fannie while Rachel waited in line for the water. Walking slowly so as not to spill, she placed the soft-sided nylon bowl in front of the dog. Fannie took a few delicate sips and then moved away. Rachel emptied the bowl and folded it up, putting it in her backpack along with Fannie's ball and brush, and the special organic dog treats that the mayor's housekeeper baked each week with whole wheat flour and low-fat cheese!

"Where to?" asked Lindy. "The playground?"

"No! We can't go there!"

"Oh, right!" said Lindy, smacking her forehead. "There are children there!"

"How about the outdoor band shell? That should be empty, and Fannie could run up and down the aisles."

"Perfect!" The two girls headed down a stone path that led to the northern edge of the park. Fannie followed happily, sniffing and wagging her tail and taking in all the sights.

"She acts as if she's never been in this park," said Lindy. "Do you think that's possible?"

"Very possible. I bet the mayor only walks Fannie on her own property, so they don't run into any children."

As they approached the band shell, Lindy let out a low groan.

"What's the matter?" Rachel asked.

"Look! It must be the summer camp rehearsing a play!" She pointed to the stage, where a woman was addressing a large group of children.

"And they're in costume!" whispered Rachel. She instinctively grabbed Fannie and backed away.

"*Peter Pan*, I think," said Lindy, who had moved in closer for a better view. "Look, there's Captain Hook and Wendy and — "

"Not Captain Hook!" cried Rachel. "Remember the kid dressed like a pirate who poked Fannie with his sword? We'd better get out of here — NOW!"

"Wait," said Lindy. "Wait a minute. Look, Fannie's not even barking."

Sure enough, Fannie sat happily in Rachel's arms, not alarmed in the least. "Everything's fine," Rachel whispered to the dog. "You're safe with us."

"Hey!" said Lindy. "Let's do an experiment."

"What kind of experiment?" Rachel's voice was filled with doubt.

"Let's just sit down here, in the very back row, and hold Fannie. We can watch for a few minutes and see if the costumes upset her. And if they do — well, we'll just leave in a hurry."

Rachel wasn't sure about this. The last thing she wanted was a repeat of the evening in her driveway. But she had to admit, Fannie didn't seem bothered at all. The girls walked quietly over to the bleacher seats and sat down.

"Listen, Lost Boys!" the director called. "I need all of you to stay stage left while Peter makes his entrance. And then when Captain Hook comes on, you exit stage right, screaming in fright, okay?"

"Okay," the children chorused enthusiastically. They were clearly having a wonderful time.

"So far so good," said Lindy, stroking Fannie's back. Fannie was alert and watching the action, but she didn't seem frightened.

The Lost Boys, many of whom were little girls,

arranged themselves in a clump. They were
dressed in tattered shirts and their feet were bare.
Their faces were smudged with makeup to look
like dirt and their hair was spiked with gel.

"Enter Peter Pan!" called the director. A girl
with short hair, wearing a typical green Peter Pan
costume, made an eager entrance. The Lost Boys
ran to greet her, jumping up and down.

"Get ready," whispered Rachel. "Captain Hook
is coming next!"

The girls watched the stage, both petting Fannie
at the same time. They were shocked when a tall
boy, waving his sword, rushed right by them down
the aisle instead of entering from backstage. "Stop!"
he commanded, perching on the step right next to
the girls. "Peter Pan, I challenge you to a duel!"

Fannie barked sharply, drawing the attention
of the children onstage. "Look!" cried one. "A
puppy!"

All eyes turned to stare at Lindy, Rachel, and
Fannie. "Okay," said the director. "We need to
keep going! Attention, please!"

"Let's go!" hissed Rachel, standing up and keeping a tight grip on Fannie. "This could be a disaster."

Lindy followed her, waving back at the cast of *Peter Pan*. "Have a great show!" she called.

When they had reached what they guessed was a safe distance from the band shell, Rachel put Fannie down on the grass. "That was close."

"It was fine!" Lindy said. "Fannie did fine! She wasn't even scared. She just watched!"

Rachel thought for a moment. "You're right. She really didn't act afraid at all."

"See — that proves your theory. If we act calm, then Fannie will be calm. Mayor Mussel makes her all crazy."

Rachel looked at her watch. "It's time to go. We only have an hour before our afternoon dogs. And I'm starving!"

"Me too," said Lindy. "Let's get a snack from one of the vendors."

The girls led Fannie out of the park, careful to navigate her around groups of children riding bikes. Near the edge of the park stood four food carts with brightly colored umbrellas.

"What do you want?" asked Lindy. "Hot dogs, burritos, ice cream, or popcorn?"

"Popcorn," said Rachel. "And some lemonade. How about you?"

"I'm going to have a hot dog. That'll be my lunch." The girls dug in their pockets for change and stood in line. When they'd made their purchases, they found an empty bench and sat down.

While taking her first bite of hot dog, Lindy happened to glance down at Fannie. The dog sat at attention at Rachel's feet, not taking her eyes off of Rachel. She watched intently as Rachel's hand went from her popcorn box to her mouth.

"Look," said Lindy, pointing to the dog.

"Oh, I forgot!" said Rachel. "Popcorn! It's her favorite food!"

"Look at her! I've never seen a dog stare like that."

"And with those pleading eyes!"

"Should we give her some?" Lindy asked.

"The mayor said we could give her a handful, remember?" Rachel took a few kernels and held them out to Fannie. The dog lunged for them and devoured them quickly. Then she stared up at Rachel again, begging for more.

"It's hard to resist those eyes," said Lindy. "Give her just a couple more."

"Okay, but I don't want her to get sick. Remember, Mayor Mussel said she has a nervous stomach or something like that." Just the same, Rachel gave the dog a few more bites.

And as they stood up to leave, a piece of popcorn fell from Rachel's lap. Fannie dived for it, yanking the leash out of Lindy's hand.

"Come here, Fannie," Lindy said with a laugh. "Time for your afternoon snooze in the backyard. You've had enough excitement for one day."

"Can you believe how much she likes popcorn?" Rachel asked as they headed toward the mayor's office, so Mayor Mussel could wave at her dog from the window.

"I've never seen anything like that! We sure know what her weak spot is, don't we?"

Fannie walked between the girls, her head high and her short tail wagging. She didn't seem anything like the wriggly, tense animal who had visited Rachel's house a few nights before.

"You're such a good girl, Fannie!" Lindy praised. "I think this is going to be easy, after all."

"Then you can check her *auditory canals* when we get to my house," joked Rachel.

As they passed the mayor's office, the girls saw that the mayor was standing on the front steps waiting for them. "Are we late?" asked Rachel, hoping very much that they weren't.

"No," admitted Mayor Mussel. "I was just eager to see how things went."

"They went fine," said Lindy with a pleased smile. "Just fine."

Mayor Mussel reached down and picked up Fannie. "How's my baby Fannie? How's my precious little dog? Did you have a nice time in the park?"

Fannie licked the mayor on her nose, which made Mayor Mussel laugh. Rachel realized she'd never heard the mayor laugh before — the sound of it was almost a shock.

"And what did you do in the park, Fannie-wannie? Did you play ball?"

"Not exactly," said Lindy honestly. "Fannie just liked watching all the — the *action* around her."

Rachel was hoping that Lindy didn't plan to tell her about watching *Peter Pan*. She had a feeling such news wouldn't sit well with Mayor Mussel. It was only their first day working for the mayor, and Rachel wanted her to trust them.

"Yes," said the mayor. "I don't usually walk Fannie in the park. Too many people. And children."

SEVEN

Fannie Escapes!

On Friday, the third of July, Cove Beach, California, experienced one of the hottest days of the summer season. The temperature soared to 101 degrees. The sandy beaches were so crowded they looked like a shimmering carpet of humans, striped umbrellas, blankets, and coolers.

But Lindy and Rachel weren't among the surfers and sunbathers cooling off in the ocean. They were dutifully taking Fannie for her afternoon walk in Cove Beach Park. Only this time, Lindy had brought along her own dog, Sam, who had been acting as if he felt neglected.

"Now that we have Fannie's care down to a science," Lindy told Rachel, "I don't think it will be a problem to bring Sam along. He's been feeling so sad lately."

"Not to mention hot!" added Rachel. "Look at him panting."

"We'll find some shade in the park. And give the dogs a drink." Lindy took Sam's leash, while Rachel walked with Fannie.

When they reached the center of the park, both dogs pulled toward the statue fountain. Unknown to Mayor Mussel, Fannie now preferred to take her drinks there with the other dogs. After only a day of sipping from her collapsible bowl, she had followed the lead of her fellow canines and lapped right from the cool water of the marble fountain.

"Mayor Mussel would have a fit!" said Rachel, watching Fannie take a long, happy drink. "All that bacteria!"

"But Fannie made up her own mind to drink from the fountain," replied Lindy with a shrug. "There's not much we can do about that."

"True," said Rachel. "I can't believe how relaxed Fannie seems after just a few days with us.

Do you think it's a coincidence, or do you think we've been a good influence on her?"

Lindy stopped to pet Fannie. She had grown used to seeing the compact black dog walking eagerly beside them, alert and curious — and yes, relaxed! "I don't think it's a coincidence. I think your theory is right. We've been very matter-of-fact around Fannie, and that's how she's behaved."

"You know," said Rachel, "I found this book about dogs at home, and I looked at it last night. Know what it said about English Cocker Spaniels?"

"What?"

"Well, the part about them needing lots of daily exercise is true. But the book also said that they are loyal, affectionate, and make wonderful companion dogs."

"Fannie is definitely all those things," agreed Lindy.

"But here's the amazing thing. The book said Cocker Spaniels are *good with children*!"

"Really?" asked Lindy, amazed. "It said that?"

"Yep. It even showed a picture of three little kids holding one — and the dog looked pretty happy."

Lindy reached down to pet Fannie. "Is this true, that you like children? Have you been fooling everybody all this time?"

Fannie licked Lindy's palm, wagging her tail as though agreeing.

"Fannie has been just fine around children here in the park," noted Rachel. "And she actually does well around other dogs. Look at her with Sam! I just wish we could make Mayor Mussel believe that."

"But we're out of time now. Our job with Fannie ends after this walk," said Lindy. "And you know something? I'm going to miss her."

"Me too," said Rachel. "She's a great dog. But these past few days have been a lot of work!"

"I know," Lindy agreed. "I'm pooped! We made a lot of money, though!"

Rachel smiled, thinking once again about riding lessons in the fall. But she, too, would miss the sweet Cocker Spaniel. "I wonder if the mayor is going to bring Fannie to the barbecue tonight?"

Lindy smiled with delight. She'd almost forgotten the Fourth of July barbecue, to be held that evening right in the park! Her whole family was going, and so was Rachel's. "Probably not, Rach. Too many children."

"That's right. And her housekeeper comes back from her trip tonight. So, Fanny will probably have to stay at the glass house on top of the hill, bored stiff."

"Hey, Sam!" said Lindy. "Stop pulling me!"

After their cool drink, both Sam and Fannie seemed to want to play. "It's too hot to play ball," said Rachel. "I'm sweating just standing here."

"Let's take them over by the soccer fields," suggested Lindy. "I bet it's pretty empty over there, and we could let them run. We don't want to return Fannie to Mayor Mussel without exercising her properly!"

Luckily, the soccer fields were deserted. "I

think everyone's at the beach," said Rachel, removing Fannie's leash.

Fannie immediately took off running — as fast as her short legs could go. Lindy unleashed Sam, who ran happily after Fannie.

"Here!" shouted Rachel, throwing a yellow tennis ball for the dogs. "Go get it!"

Both dogs veered off toward the ball, but Fannie reached it first.

"She's fast for a little thing," Lindy said, laughing. "Look at her go!"

Fannie brought the ball back, covered with saliva. "Yuck!" said Rachel, throwing it again. "Slobber ball!"

This time Sam got the ball. Rachel and Lindy played catch with the dogs for another ten minutes, until both dogs were panting. "Okay, that's enough running in this heat," said Rachel. "Let's get your leashes back on and go get another drink."

"And one for me," said Lindy, wiping her forehead with the back of her hand.

Just then, a group of older kids spilled onto the far end of the soccer field, tossing a purple Frisbee back and forth. They drank from cans of soda, talking and laughing together. Loud rock music blared from a portable radio carried by a tall, barefoot boy.

"High school alert!" said Lindy, grinning.

"Do you think we'll act goofy like that when we're in high school?" asked Rachel, watching the older girls and boys dance together in a line near the soccer net.

While Lindy considered this question, Fannie suddenly took off running toward the animated group. "Fannie!" called Rachel. "Fannie, come back here! Come, Fannie!"

"Oh, no!" cried Lindy. She grabbed for Sam, hooking his leash quickly.

"I'll go get her." Rachel ran after Fannie, not stopping to pick up the dog's bright pink leash. Nearly out of breath, she arrived just in time to see what had enticed the dog — the kids were eating cheese popcorn from a huge plastic bag!

Could Fannie have smelled the popcorn all the way across the field? she wondered as she stopped to catch her breath. "Fannie, come here!" Rachel tried to keep her voice calm so Fannie wouldn't get upset.

But Fannie didn't seem too upset — she was busy gobbling up every single spilled piece of popcorn. With great intensity, she lunged for each bright orange kernel that landed on the ground.

"Is this your dog?" asked a girl with spiky blonde hair and sunglasses.

"No," Rachel explained. "My friend and I are pet-sitting."

"Cool," said the girl. "She's a cutie!"

"And she definitely craves popcorn," noted the boy carrying the radio. "Look at her — she's crazy for it." He tossed a handful toward Fannie. His friends joined in, laughing hysterically as Fannie dove for the cheese-coated treats.

Rachel tried not to be intimidated by the older kids. But she knew she had to get Fannie away

from the popcorn. "She's Mayor Mussel's dog and — I have to take her back now."

"You're kidding!"

"Really?"

"Wow, the mayor's dog!"

"Little Mussel Dog!"

"Does the dog get to vote?"

The kids were laughing and making jokes, but Rachel could tell they liked Fannie. And Fannie liked them, because they kept petting her and feeding her more and more popcorn.

I better get Fannie out of here before all this popcorn gives her an upset stomach, thought Rachel. "Come here, Fannie. We have to go." She leaned down and picked up the little dog, cradling her tightly in her arms. Fannie tried to squirm loose, but Rachel kept her firm grip.

"Nice to meet you, Mussel Dog," the kids said. "Give our regards to the mayor." They waved and laughed some more, as if this were the funniest thing they had ever encountered.

And as Rachel turned to leave, she felt a few popcorn kernels hit her bare ankles. "Let's go," she whispered to Fannie. "You've had your fill of popcorn, I think."

Fannie licked Rachel's face, energized by the food and the company of the doting teenagers.

"Well, she's not afraid of older kids, that's for sure," Rachel told Lindy when they returned. "She was in heaven. And I'm so hot I think I'm going to fall down."

"What were they doing?" asked Lindy.

"Feeding her cheese popcorn."

"Oh, no wonder," said Lindy, petting the dog. "Aren't you the lucky pooch today?"

"Just don't mention it to Mayor Mussel," said Rachel. "The kids were being really nice to Fannie, but she might not like the idea of her dog eating popcorn with a bunch of teenagers."

Lindy turned around to watch the teens leave the field. Sweat ran down her neck and trickled onto her back. "I can't stand this heat! Shall we go? Maybe we can go to the beach for a little while before the barbecue." She gave Sam's leash a gentle tug.

Rachel held Fannie against her left hip with one arm, leaning down to pick up the leash with the other. She thought she had a firm grip on the little spaniel, but somehow Fannie wriggled free and leaped to the ground. She ran full speed toward the other end of the soccer field, her short legs moving at double speed.

"Oh, no!" cried Rachel. "Not again!"

"Fannie, come back!" cried Lindy. "It's HOT!"

"I can't believe her!" Rachel shouted, running after the dog for the second time. "She wants more of that popcorn."

Rachel could see Fannie stop in the spot where the kids had been, her nose to the ground. She searched for any remaining crumbs, moving in an arc across the area.

"Fannie, come!" Rachel shouted as she drew closer. "Come here, girl! Let's go!"

But instead of coming, Fannie trotted in the opposite direction, following a trail of popcorn crumbs left by the teens. Rachel ran faster, trying not to panic. This was the first time Fannie hadn't come when called. It wasn't like her to go off on her own — she always stayed pretty close to her humans.

Rachel could hear Lindy shouting behind her, but she couldn't make out the words. And she couldn't stop! She had to keep going until she caught up with Fannie. She couldn't let herself think of anything but pursuing the spaniel and returning her to the mayor.

"Come, Fannie!" Rachel shouted until her throat burned. But at the end of the soccer field, Fannie disappeared down a hill and into an area of the park dense with trees. Rachel's heart suddenly exploded with fear. Fannie was nowhere in sight. *This can't be happening!* she thought.

Rachel turned around and motioned frantically for Lindy and Sam to follow. "Fannie's gone!" she shouted. "We have to find her!"

Lindy bounded across the open field, Sam beside her. "Where'd she go?"

"Into the trees! Come on!"

"Oh, no!" Lindy cried. "Fannie! Fannie!"

Sam headed for the trees, picking up on Fannie's scent. He practically dragged Lindy behind, but she didn't care.

"Fannie!" she shouted over and over. "Fannie, come here!"

"Please come back!" Rachel called. *Please! Or we're doomed!*

EIGHT

The Search Is On

"I can't go any farther," said Lindy. She leaned over to catch her breath by the statue fountain. "I'm drenched in sweat."

"I really need a drink of water," said Rachel. "How long have we been searching?"

Lindy looked at her watch. "About twenty minutes, I think. Where could Fannie have gone? We've looked everywhere."

Rachel shook her head. She couldn't even think straight. "She has to be here somewhere. We can't give up."

"What should we do?" Lindy asked. "When Sam wanders off, he always finds his way home. But we're pretty far from the mayor's house."

"As much as I hate to say it, I think we should

go to the mayor's office and tell her that Fannie wandered off."

Lindy groaned and closed her eyes. "She's going to be so mad!"

"I know. But if we don't get some help, we're never going to find Fannie. We can't waste any more time." Rachel shielded her eyes and looked around.

"Aren't you scared to tell Mayor Mussel what happened? What if she gets mad at our parents, too?"

"Up until today," said Rachel, "L & R Leash had a perfect record. We never had a dog injured, or sick, or — lost. Everyone trusted us to take good care of their animals."

"It wasn't our fault exactly," Lindy replied. Her voice was thick with fatigue and frustration.

"Still — we were in charge. We even signed a contract."

"Oh, no!" cried Lindy. "I completely forgot we signed that stupid contract! My father will be furious that I signed something legal without his advice!"

"And you know what's worse? We didn't even

read it that day at the beach. It was hot, and my mom was waiting in the car and — "

"And," finished Lindy, "we stopped thinking the minute Mayor Mussel told us we were going to make twenty-five dollars a day. I never even showed the contract to my dad, like Mayor Mussel told us to do!"

Rachel dug the toe of her tennis shoe into the dirt. "I hate to say this," she said, looking at her friend, "but you were the one who wanted to take on an extra dog. Even after you promised me we wouldn't."

Lindy stared at Rachel, her jaw dropping. "Do you mean to say you're blaming this on *me*? That's not fair! You're the one who let Fannie escape!"

"I did not! She jumped out of my arms!"

Lindy's face was red with anger. She put her hands on her hips. "You're the worrywart! How come you didn't think to worry about teenagers carrying bags of cheese popcorn!"

Rachel started to respond but then stopped. Instead, she burst out laughing.

"What's so funny?" Lindy asked. "I don't see anything funny!"

"Think about it," said Rachel. "How could even the best worrywart in the world predict that cheese popcorn could be dangerous?"

Lindy thought about it, and a smile spread slowly across her face. "You're right. I'm sorry. I'm just so — worried! There, I said it. I'm WORRIED."

"I know." Rachel nodded. "But take it from an expert — worry doesn't help anything. We have to stay calm and think clearly."

"Let's go tell our parents — and Mayor Mussel," said Lindy. "Come on, Sam." Sam sat up slowly, tired and hot from searching the park.

As the two girls and the drooping dog headed out of the park toward Main Street, Rachel put her arm through Lindy's. "I'm sorry, Lindy. I don't want to fight with you. It's nobody's fault. It just happened."

Lindy was quiet for a moment, watching for traffic before they crossed the street. "You know something? You and I have never really had a fight before. I don't think I like it."

"We can't let this ruin our friendship," said Rachel.

"We won't," promised Lindy.

"And we're going to find Fannie, I just know it!" Rachel thought it was kind of strange to be the one who felt more confident and less worried. That was always Lindy's position. Oh, the situation was serious, no question. But for some reason, Rachel felt more focused on solving the problem that faced them.

"Do you want me to go in?" Rachel asked Lindy. "I don't mind."

Lindy looked toward the door of the mayor's office. She cleared her throat. "I guess I should stay out here with Sam."

"Okay," Rachel agreed. She took a deep breath and approached the front door. "Wish me luck."

"Luck," whispered Lindy, crossing her fingers and holding them up high.

Rachel pushed open the heavy door and disappeared inside. Lindy watched her go, admiring her friend's sudden burst of courage.

Inside, Rachel looked around quickly, wondering who she would see first. But the place seemed strangely quiet. She tiptoed past the open door of the mayor's office and found that no one was inside. Jill and Tom weren't in their offices, either. Finally, she approached the conference room, hoping with all her heart that an important meeting wasn't in progress. The door was ajar, and Rachel could hear the murmur of voices, though she couldn't make them out.

She peeked around the edge of the door and couldn't believe what she saw. There, at the long table stood Jill and Tom, wearing aprons and plastic gloves and cutting watermelons into thick, juicy slabs. They talked comfortably with each other, stacking the fruit on huge trays.

"Hi," Rachel said in a quiet voice. Both Tom and Jill looked up, startled by the noise.

"Rachel!" said Jill.

"Hi, honey!" said Tom. His smile was warm and he looked happy to see her.

"We were wondering when you were going to get here," said Jill. "Where's Lindy?"

"Outside with Sam."

"Is something wrong?" Tom studied Rachel's face carefully.

"Well," began Rachel, trying to think where to start, "we had a little — " And then her voice broke.

Tom took off his plastic gloves and put an arm around Rachel. "What happened, sweetheart?"

"We lost Fannie!" Rachel said in a burst.

Jill gasped and came hurrying over. "What happened?"

"Before I explain," Rachel said, "please promise you won't be mad at me and Lindy, because we really need your help."

"Of course," said Tom, squeezing Rachel's shoulders. "We're here."

"Is the mayor here?" asked Rachel. "Because she should hear this, too."

"Well," replied Jill, "it's kind of a long story, but no — she's not here."

"Where is Fannie, Rachel?" Tom asked kindly.

"She got away from us in the park when we were playing on the soccer field. We looked all over and we can't find her!"

"Oh, no!" said Jill. "Where is Lindy?"

"Outside with Sam," Rachel explained. "She's pretty upset."

Tom gave Rachel an understanding pat on the back.

"I'm so sorry, Tom," Rachel said. She felt tears stinging her eyes. "We didn't mean to. We've been so careful with all the dogs, but Fannie saw some teenagers with cheese popcorn and they were feeding her and then — "

"Shh," said Tom, giving her a hug. "The important thing right now is to find Fannie. I'm going to call Mom to let her know where we are. Wait for me outside and then we'll get going."

"Back to the park?"

"It wouldn't hurt to go back once more and

check. Then, if we don't find her, we'll branch out."

Rachel smiled up at Tom, filled with relief at how helpful and understanding he was being. "You know what?" she said. "You're really great. You're a really great — dad — to me."

"And you're a really great daughter, Rachel." He kissed her on top of her head and went over to the phone in the corner.

"What about all the watermelon? What will you do with it?"

"It'll be fine here until the barbecue tonight," Tom said.

But Rachel wondered if any of them would be able to go to the festivities in Cove Beach Park that night, or if they would still be looking for Fannie.

"Did you tell Mayor Mussel?" Lindy's face was flushed and serious, and she clutched Sam's leash with a tight grip.

"She wasn't in there. But I told your mom and Tom."

"Are they mad?"

Rachel shook her head. "They were both really nice. They're going to lock up and come help us."

"Whew!" breathed Lindy. "I couldn't figure out what was taking so long. I was getting worried."

"Isn't it a weird coincidence that the mayor is gone?"

Lindy nodded. "You don't suppose Fannie would have followed one of those teenagers home, do you?"

"I told them that Fannie was the mayor's dog," Rachel remembered. "I think if one of them had found her, they would have brought her back by now."

"You're right. But Fannie was so crazy for that cheese popcorn."

Tom and Jill came out of the office, locking the door behind them. Tom reached down and patted Sam on the head. "Well, we have at least one piece of luck on our side, girls."

"What?" Lindy couldn't think of anything lucky except finding Fannie.

"I just checked my messages, and Mayor Mussel called. She left this morning to drive up the coast to check on her mother, who is ill. She had planned to drive back later this afternoon, but she decided to spend the night and take care of some things."

Rachel wasn't sure she understood. "So?"

"So, in her message she asked the two of you to keep Fannie until the morning."

"She's going to miss the barbecue?" Jill asked.

Tom nodded. "We're supposed to manage things for her."

"She doesn't know Fannie is lost?" Lindy asked.

"Not yet," said Tom. "She's going to call us at home later, Rachel, to check in."

"Oh, no!" cried Rachel.

"What will we tell her?" Lindy mused, pacing the sidewalk.

"Well," said Jill, "let's go find Fannie before the mayor calls back and asks about her."

"It's already a quarter to four," Lindy announced.

"And the barbecue is at seven," added Jill. "Tom and I still have a lot to do."

"Then let's hurry," said Tom. "Let's go back to the park."

"We looked everywhere in the park already!" Lindy cried.

"But she's a little dog," reminded Tom. "She could fit into a lot of small spaces."

"You're right," Rachel said, thinking of the bushes and trees. "I hope she's not scared, poor thing."

"Remember," added Tom, "dogs are very smart creatures. And they have an instinct for survival. Let's just think positively, okay?"

"Besides," said Jill with a smile, "there are certain advantages to working for the mayor."

"Like what, Mom?"

Jill held out a ring of keys. "I can open the maintenance shed and borrow one of the electric carts that the gardeners use. We can drive it all around the park to look for Fannie."

"Good idea!" said Tom. "But what about old Sam here?"

Jill glanced down at poor, tired Sam. "We should leave him in my office, Lindy, where it's nice and cool. We'll come back for him later."

"You're right," Lindy agreed. "He deserves a rest." She took him inside and made sure he had water to drink.

Back on the sidewalk, Rachel waited impatiently, trying not to think of the dangers Fannie might be encountering that very second.

"Let's go!" said Lindy, reappearing. Her voice sounded surprisingly shaky and small.

"We're coming, Fannie!" called Rachel, trying to add some confidence to her own voice. "The search party is coming!"

NINE

The Search Continues

"Turn left!" said Lindy. "Let's go back to the soccer fields!" She sat next to her mother, who expertly guided the maintenance cart through Cove Beach Park. In the back, Tom and Rachel kept a lookout for the small black spaniel.

"I don't see her," said Rachel, shielding her eyes.

"Let's take the path through the trees that leads to the pond," suggested Tom.

As they passed the picnic area, they noticed a group of workers preparing for the evening's festivities. The men and women volunteers were cleaning grills, hanging lights, and setting out stacks of paper plates and utensils. But there was no Fannie to be seen.

"I think we should call it quits in the park," said Jill. She stopped the cart and got out to stretch her legs. "We've been everywhere."

"Where else should we look?" asked Lindy.

"I'm not sure," Jill admitted. "Got any ideas, Tom?"

Tom stroked his chin and thought for a moment. "I believe this calls for a more organized search effort."

"What do you mean?" asked Rachel.

"Well, we need more people to cover a larger area."

"You're right!" said Jill. "I'll call Mrs. West. Maybe she can put Shelby in the wagon and pull her around our neighborhood, in case Fannie went back there."

"Great," said Rachel. "And maybe my mom can take Luke along in the stroller and help look."

Lindy jumped out of the cart, excited. "Let's call my dad, too. I'll bet he'll put on his Rollerblades and go all over town."

"Yes!" cried Rachel, giving Lindy a high five.

Jill pulled a cellular phone out of her back pocket. "Let's call everyone and get going. I'll take the girls in the cart and head down by the beach."

"I'll go on foot up and down Main," said Tom. "I think we should agree to meet back in front of the mayor's office in one hour. Okay?"

"Okay," said Jill.

Rachel felt a thousand times better now that an organized plan had been put into motion. Maybe with everyone helping, they would find Fannie and this whole, terrible ordeal would be over.

"You know what, Mom?" said Lindy. "You and Tom are pretty smart. No wonder Mayor Mussel likes having you on her team."

"Thanks, honey." Jill smiled, clearly delighted by the compliment.

"And we have smart daughters," added Tom.

"Until today," said Rachel with a frown. "Until we lost the most famous dog in Cove Beach."

"Everyone makes mistakes," Tom assured the girls. "We'll find Fannie."

"We have to," said Rachel and Lindy, almost at the same time.

But an hour later, the tired search party met back in front of the mayor's office, looking sweaty and disappointed.

"She's not on Main Street," said Tom. "I've been up and down six times."

"And we didn't see her at the beach," put in Lindy.

Mrs. West, the Martinezes' baby-sitter, rubbed her hand. "I have a blister from pulling the wagon. No sign of that dog where I looked."

"Me either," said Gwen, looking down at baby Luke, who was asleep in the stroller.

"Where's Dad?" asked Lindy.

Jill scanned the street. "Not back yet, I guess."

"Well, what do we do now?" asked Rachel.

Tom looked at his watch. "I'm concerned about the barbecue. We're losing time."

"There's Dad!" screamed Lindy, pointing down the street. A man in a purple helmet skated up the

street, coming to a perfect stop next to his daughter.

"Did you see Fannie, Dad?"

Rob Martinez unhooked the strap of his helmet and took it off. "No," he said, running a hand through his dark hair. "And I even went up to Mayor Mussel's house to see if Fannie tried to make it home."

"Darn!" said Lindy, snapping her fingers impatiently.

"But there has been a Fannie sighting, I'm happy to report," Rob continued.

"Where?" cried everyone in unison.

"I stopped by the police station to ask if any of the patrol officers had seen her."

"And?" prompted Lindy, unable to contain her excitement.

"And an Officer Walters said he saw a dog fitting Fannie's description heading south on Second Avenue about an hour ago."

"Really?" said Tom. "Second Avenue."

"What's there that Fannie would like?" mused

Rachel. "I think we should try thinking like a Cocker Spaniel."

"Rachel, that's brilliant!" yelled Lindy. "We've been thinking like humans."

"Speak for yourself," joked Rob.

Lindy grabbed Rachel's hand. "We need to put ourselves in Fannie's shoes and — "

"Fannie doesn't wear shoes," interrupted Shelby from the back of the red wagon.

"I know, Shelby. I just meant that in order to find Fannie, we need to think about what she likes and where she likes to go."

"Well," began Rachel, "she's very curious."

"And energetic," added Lindy.

"And temperamental," said Tom.

"And afraid of children," said Gwen, looking down at Luke.

"Actually," Rachel put in, "she's not. Mayor Mussel just thinks she is, so then Fannie acts that way."

"Right," explained Lindy. "While she's been with us, she's been calm and friendly."

"Well," said Tom, "then that's quite an accomplishment, I'd say. You've been good for Fannie."

"If you don't count losing her," sighed Rachel.

"Popcorn," Lindy whispered suddenly.

"What?" whispered Shelby, thinking there was a secret.

"Popcorn," Lindy said a little louder.

"Popcorn!" repeated Rachel.

"POPCORN!" shouted both girls together.

Rob shook his head. "Can someone fill me in on what popcorn has to do with Fannie?"

"Dad," said Lindy, "Fannie loves popcorn. It's her favorite food. She got away from us because some teenagers fed her popcorn."

"Yes!" continued Rachel. "We have to think about where else in Cove Beach Fannie could find popcorn to eat."

"There are the movies, of course," said Gwen. "But that's pretty obvious."

"Great," said Rachel. "We'll check both cinemas."

Jill bit her lip, thinking. "I know! The video

store. They have that popcorn machine by the checkout counter, with free popcorn."

"Right," agreed Tom. "And I think the candy store on Second Avenue sells popcorn."

"Second Avenue," said Shelby. "Isn't that where the police saw Fannie?"

"Very good, honey," said Rob, leaning down to ruffle his daughter's hair. "Maybe that's why she was over in that area."

"Where else?" wondered Mrs. West, a finger on her chin. "Oh, I know. That used-car dealer over on Fifth sometimes gives away popcorn and soft drinks."

"That's a lot of places," said Jill. "We should split up and then meet back here one more time."

"I know we're forgetting somewhere," said Rachel, tapping her toe. "But it won't come to me."

"The park!" said Lindy. "They have a popcorn cart."

Tom shook his head. "We've been past that cart three or four times."

But Rachel knew there was *another* place in Cove Beach where you could buy popcorn. *Where was it?*

Think, Rachel, think! Think about popcorn . . .

After selecting their sites, the search parties took off once again. Giving up wagons and strollers and golf carts, they decided to take cars instead. Everyone, that is, except Rob, who said he could skate faster than any car could travel in Friday holiday traffic.

Lindy and Rachel went with Tom to search the two movie theaters in Cove Beach. One was a block off Main Street. It was a small cinema that showed foreign films and documentaries.

"Have you seen a black Cocker Spaniel?" Lindy asked the woman at the ticket booth.

The woman laughed and shook her head. "I saw a woman who had a poodle haircut earlier, but no dogs."

The girls checked inside at the snack counter, but the boy working there hadn't seen any dogs, either. Just to be safe, Tom checked out the area in back, near the Dumpsters, where all the empty popcorn cartons ended up. But he returned to the car shaking his head.

At the newer multiplex cinema outside of the main area of town, they met with the same story. A uniformed guard told them that he hadn't seen any strays at all that day. "A man showed up with a Seeing Eye dog last week, but that's the only dog that's been around here."

"She's not a stray," Rachel said with great dignity. "The dog we're looking for is a purebred English Cocker Spaniel who belongs to Mayor Mussel."

"The mayor's dog?" said the guard, standing a little straighter. "You don't say!"

"I do say," said Lindy, feeling impatient.

"Is she offering a reward?"

Lindy and Rachel looked at each other. Tom stepped in and rescued the moment. "The reward would be saving a wonderful animal."

And us, thought Rachel.

"I'll be on the lookout," the guard promised.

"Now what?" asked Rachel when they had returned to the car.

"I don't know," admitted Tom. "I'm out of ideas. But let's go see what the others found out."

Once again, the looks on the faces of the search party members told the same story: no Fannie.

"We give up, don't we, Mommy?" said Shelby. "I'm hungry."

"So is Luke," said Gwen. "Can I go inside your office, Tom, and feed him?"

"And we should check on Sam," said Jill.

"I'll buy everyone a soda from the machine," offered Tom.

"I'm ready for that!" Rob leaned down and unbuckled his blades.

"I'm going to go home," Mrs. West said wearily. "If you don't need me any more today."

"That's fine," said Jill. "You've been a real help."

"What are we going to do?" Rachel asked for

about the hundredth time. She was starting to feel frightened. "What if Fannie is hurt?"

"Or scared?" said Lindy.

"What if she thinks we abandoned her?" Rachel continued. "What if she went somewhere really far away and we never — "

"Stop thinking like that," said Tom. "I bet she's really close by. Somewhere silly that we've just overlooked."

Rachel tried to feel as confident and sunny as Tom. But it was hard. "Somewhere close by . . ." she mused.

"A place we've overlooked," said Lindy, gazing up at the sky for an answer.

"A place with popcorn," finished Shelby.

The room was silent while everyone searched their collective memories of Cove Beach for the one place where Fannie might be.

TEN

Finding Fannie

"You haven't touched your food, girls," said Tom. He looked at Lindy and Rachel, sitting dejectedly at a long picnic table. "You should eat so you'll have energy to keep looking for Fannie."

Because of Tom's and Jill's duties, the girls had been forced to temporarily suspend their search and attend the picnic. Rachel stared at the grilled chicken and corn on her plate. She glanced around at the excited holiday crowd, spilling out onto the grassy areas of the park. "I'm not hungry."

"Me either," said Lindy. "And I'm definitely not in the mood to celebrate."

Rachel put her head down on her hand. "I'm so worried about Fannie. And in a couple of hours, Mayor Mussel will be calling to check on her."

"And we'll have to tell her that we lost her dog and we have no idea where she is." Lindy looked red-eyed and weary.

Though it was after seven P.M., the sun was still strong and hot. The picnic pavilion was overflowing with families who had come to join the fun at the annual Fourth of July picnic. The whole park had an air of celebration. The members of a brass band were practicing for the concert later on, and Jill was setting out trays of watermelon for the seed-spitting contest.

"I never want to be responsible for another dog again in my life," said Rachel. "It's too hard."

"I know," Lindy agreed. "I wish we'd never even thought of L & R Leash. We should have just spent the summer at the beach!"

Tom grinned and tried to look cheerful. "Now, come on, ladies. You've done a great job with your business. And you earned your own money! We're going to find that little dog, don't you worry."

"Where, though?" asked Rachel. "And how?

You and Jill need to stay here for the picnic."

"If you can think of somewhere you want to look," said Tom, "I'll take you. Jill can handle things here, now that the picnic's under way. She's going to be the next mayor, after all."

"I can't think of anywhere else to look," said Lindy. "And we already called the animal shelters."

"Maybe we should put up signs," Rachel suggested. "And offer a reward, the way that man at the movie theater wanted."

"It's too late to do that tonight," said Tom. "If we don't find her tonight, we'll make signs tomorrow."

Then Shelby and Rob appeared, balancing plates of food and glasses of lemonade. "These seats reserved?" Rob asked.

Lindy shook her head and moved down to make room for her little sister. "Your mom's doing a good job, don't you think?" Rob asked his older daughter. Lindy nodded again, too upset to talk.

Rachel nudged Lindy's foot under the table to

get her attention. Then she looked meaningfully at her friend and whispered, "Contract!"

"What?" said Lindy.

"Ask your dad about the — you-know-what!"

"What?" asked Rob, diving into his potato salad.

"Um, Dad," said Lindy, "we have a legal question to ask you."

"Okay, shoot." Rob reached over to cut Shelby's chicken for her.

"Well, the thing is, see — well, Rachel and I signed a contract with the mayor. About Fannie."

Rob turned in surprise. "You did? When was this?"

"When we agreed to take care of Fannie," Rachel answered. "She wanted everything to be legal, she said. And she wanted us to show you the contract, too, only we — "

"And what exactly did the contract say?" Rob asked. "Can you remember?"

Rachel and Lindy looked at each other. "See, Dad, the thing is . . . we didn't exactly read it. And now that we've lost the mayor's dog, I guess we could be — "

"Legally responsible for damages," Rob finished.

"What does that mean?" Rachel asked.

"It means that the mayor could make you pay money if her dog was injured or lost while in your care. Lindy, I can't believe you signed a contract without asking me about it."

"I'm sorry, Dad. It's just that we were in a hurry, and she offered us a lot of money, and — "

"And that's why the world needs lawyers," said Rob. "This could be very serious, girls. Do you realize that?"

Lindy and Rachel nodded miserably. Things were going from bad to worse.

"Is the mayor going to put Lindy and Rachel in jail?" asked Shelby, her dark eyes wide.

"No, honey," Rob assured her. "But I am concerned about this. I wish you had come to me. You should never sign anything that you haven't read carefully and understood completely."

"We know that now," Lindy said. "But it's too late."

"Where is the contract?" Rob asked.

"In my room at home," said Lindy.

"Well, I'll take a look at it later. Right now, we'd better keep thinking about where to look for the dog."

Suddenly Rachel stood up from the table, nearly falling backward. She knew the answer! She could see it all in her mind — Fannie's small, compact body, her tail wagging, her face cocked to the side with her intelligent eyes searching out the perfect source of popcorn! And Rachel could also see where that popcorn was — the one place they'd overlooked.

She let out a strange cry that sounded like something between a cough and a scream. Tom came hurrying over from the next table, where he had been talking to some friends.

"Rach! You okay, honey?"

Lindy stood up, too, worried about her friend. "Are you choking?"

Rachel shook her head. Her eyes were wide and staring and her jaw hung open. "The beach!"

"What?" asked Shelby.

"Fannie! The beach!"

"But we looked at the beach," Lindy said.

Rachel looked around from Tom to Rob to Shelby to Lindy. "But we forgot that there is a popcorn cart at the beach. We just looked around the parking lot and the sand."

"That's right," said Lindy. "That guy at the beach sells popcorn and cheese popcorn, and candy corn. Over by the rest rooms!"

"Let's go," said Tom. "I'll drive you. It's worth a try."

"But the beach will be empty," protested Rob. "Everyone in town is here for the picnic. And the food carts will be all closed up."

"Let's try!" insisted Rachel. "Please?"

"Rob, will you tell Jill and Gwen that we'll be right back?" Tom took his car keys from his pocket.

"Sure thing," said Rob. "Good luck!"

"I hope you find Fannie so you don't have to go to jail!" Shelby called after them.

The wide strip of sand at the beach was deserted except for one young couple taking pictures of the tide pools and a man jogging right along the water. Lindy and Rachel took off running toward the rest rooms and snack area, kicking up sand behind them.

Tom took off his work shoes and socks and hurried after the girls. But when they arrived near the concrete building, all they could see was a line of shiny silver food carts completely closed up for the night. And one young woman, carrying a last load of snow cone supplies from the closed cart to her car.

"Hello," said the young woman. "We're closed for the night."

"When did everyone else leave?" asked Tom politely.

"Oh, just about ten minutes ago. Everyone wants to go to the picnic."

"Have you seen a lost dog?" asked Lindy. "A little black one?"

The woman shook her head. "No, but it was pretty crazy when we were all packing up our carts. I wasn't really watching the beach."

"Well, thanks anyway," said Tom. They waved at the woman as she left the area, her arms full.

"Look at all this trash!" said Lindy. All around were crumpled paper cups, pieces of hot dogs, candy wrappers, Popsicle sticks, and — smashed popcorn kernels.

"You'd think people could reach the trash bins, since they're in plain sight," Tom complained. "I guess the maintenance crews haven't been here yet."

A brave seagull swooped down and expertly snapped up a piece of popcorn. "Fannie wouldn't have a chance here, with the seagulls," said Rachel. "They seem to like popcorn, too."

"I don't see her anywhere," said Lindy. "But it was a good idea."

"I think we'll have to call it quits for tonight," said Tom.

"But we can't give up!" cried Rachel. "We have to find her!"

The jogger ran past them, toward the parking lot. Lindy called after him. "Excuse me, sir! Have you seen a little black dog?"

The man turned around and stopped, looking at the girls. "A little dog? Cocker Spaniel?"

"Yes!" said both girls at once.

"I did see one earlier. I thought he was with a family, because a couple of kids were playing with him."

"Where'd they go?" asked Tom.

"Don't know. Sorry," puffed the man, continuing his jog.

"She was here!" said Rachel.

"That couldn't have been Fannie," said Tom. "That guy said the dog was playing with some kids."

"But that's what we've been trying to tell you,"

said Lindy. "She's not afraid of children. Mayor Mussel just thinks she is, so she keeps Fannie away from them."

"Okay," said Tom, thinking. "Well, maybe this family went off to the picnic and took Fannie with them."

"You mean we should go back to the park?" said Rachel. "We're going in circles."

"I know," said Tom. "But do you have a better idea?"

"No," said Lindy.

The three turned to go back to the parking lot. But suddenly, they heard a strange sound.

Orf-orf.

"Did you hear that?" asked Rachel.

"Yeah," said Lindy. She stopped to listen again. "It's coming from — from one of the carts."

Once again they heard a high-pitched *orf-orf-orf.* "You don't think . . ." said Lindy, looking at Rachel.

"Couldn't be. No way. How could a dog get inside a — "

Orf-orf. Orf-orf-orf.

Even Tom looked startled now. He walked over to the row of carts, listening carefully. He stopped in front of one, leaned down, and knocked on the side.

Orf-orf-orf.

"That's Fannie!" cried Rachel. "That's her bark!"

"Oh, no!" shouted Lindy. "How'd she get in there?"

"And how will we get her out?" asked Rachel. "Fannie, Fannie! Can you hear us? It's going to be all right, Fannie!"

"I have no idea who owns these carts," said a bewildered Tom. "Or how to get in touch with them."

"The owner is probably at the picnic. We could go back and make an announcement," Lindy suggested.

"No time for that," said Tom. He took his phone out of his pocket and dialed 911. "This is a job for the Cove Beach Rescue Squad."

Tom spoke quickly into the phone, and before he had even hung up, the girls could hear the piercing sound of a fire truck. "They'll know what to do," Tom said confidently. "They have the equipment to get inside and let Fannie out."

"But how did she get in?" Rachel asked. "Do you think she has enough air to breathe?"

"Look, here's an air hole! I imagine she jumped in when the folks were closing their carts."

"Probably in search of food," said Lindy. "I bet this is the popcorn cart, you wait and see."

Just then, they spotted the fire engine pulling up. Two men came running, one with a black tool-box. "Over here!" shouted Lindy. "Over here!"

The girls watched anxiously as one of the men bent down and used a thin, sharp tool to open the padlock that bound the two large doors to the cart. As he opened the door, Lindy and Rachel crowded next to him. Sure enough, they saw a quick flash of black, curled up tightly in the corner.

"Fannie!" said Rachel. "You're alive!"

The dog looked at Rachel and then sprang out

of the small space. Rachel pulled Fannie into her arms, tears streaming down her face. Lindy came close and hugged her from the other side.

Fannie was panting hard and was obviously hot. But she seemed just the same as she usually did — cute and full of personality.

"I don't think she's been in there for more than fifteen minutes," said the younger firefighter. "I think she's okay. Probably a little scared."

"And pretty thirsty," added Rachel.

"That's the weirdest sight I've ever seen," said the other firefighter. "And I've seen a lot of weird things in this town over the years."

"You gave us a real scare," said Lindy, kissing Fannie's head.

"I never want to go through that again," whispered Rachel. She went over to Tom and buried her head in his chest. "Thanks, Dad. You're the best."

It wasn't until much later that Rachel realized she'd called Tom *Dad* and meant it with all her heart.

"We'll have a lot of explaining to do when the mayor calls tonight," said Lindy, still clutching Fannie tightly.

"But at least your story has a happy ending," said Tom.

"I doubt she'll hire us ever again," said Lindy.

"I don't know about that," noted Tom. "Look at how calm Fannie is, even after her ordeal. You girls have been an excellent influence on her, and I'll tell Gretta that myself."

"Well," said Rachel as they walked back to the car, "next summer I think we really have to make it a policy not to take care of any dogs at all during the Fourth of July week. It's too hot and crazy."

Lindy stopped, frozen. She stared at her best friend. "What do you mean — *next summer*?"

Rachel started to laugh. "What's the matter, Lindy? Are you being a worrywart? We'll be fine! L & R Leash Service can handle twenty dogs next summer, no problem! Stop being such a worry-wart!"

Once Lindy realized that Rachel was teasing, she laughed, too.

The girls giggled all the way to the car, while Fannie licked Lindy's face and neck, delighted to be back with her two favorite girls.

"You know what I love about Cocker Spaniels?" said Rachel.

"Everything!" guessed Lindy as Fannie continued to lick her.

"They love a good party," Rachel explained. "They love people and good times and children and — "

"Popcorn!" added Tom.

"So let's go back to the party," finished Rachel. "We have to hear the band and spit some watermelon seeds. Let's go, Lindy!"

"Let's go, Fannie," said Tom.

"Let's go, Dad," said Rachel, taking his hand in hers. "This may be the best Fourth of July of my life, and I haven't even seen the fireworks yet!"

Facts About
English Cocker Spaniels

1. The English Cocker Spaniel most likely originated in Spain in the fourteenth century.
2. By the eighteenth century there were many types of spaniels across the world, but only two main types in England: springers, which were larger and hunted waterfowl; and cockers, which hunted woodcock.
3. Because of their early breeding, English Cocker Spaniels love to retrieve. They can cover ground quickly and flush out game for hunters.
4. They are also highly valued as companion dogs, and are loyal, devoted, affectionate pets.

5. The famous writer Rudyard Kipling had an English Cocker Spaniel, which he called his greatest fan.

6. Adult dogs weigh between 26 and 32 pounds, with females having an average height of 15–16 inches and males an average of 16–17 inches.

7. The coat is medium long all over the body, but rather short and fine on the head.

8. English Cocker Spaniels come in many colors, including solids and parti-colors in black, red, liver, orange, or golden. The most popular color is roan.

9. The English Cocker Spaniel differs from the American Cocker Spaniel in that it has more prominent eyes, with a longer muzzle and a flatter head.

10. The English Cocker Spaniel is a bit taller and heavier than the American.

11. They love to play, love to be exercised, and are very good with children!

These facts were gathered from two sources:

1. *The Reader's Digest Illustrated Book of Dogs*, 2nd ed. rev., Pleasantville, New York: The Reader's Digest Association, 1993.

2. *English Cocker Spaniels*, www.k9web.com

About the Author

Growing up in Denver, Colorado, Coleen Hubbard liked to write and put on plays in her backyard. As an adult, she still writes plays. She also now writes for children and young adults. Among her works are four books in the Treasured Horses series, which sparked her interest in writing fun books about animals and kids.

Coleen and her husband have three dog-crazy young daughters, plus Maggie the Magnificent, a sweet-natured mixed breed who inspired Coleen to learn all about the various breeds of dogs featured in the Dog Tales series.